CAT SEBASTIAN

Daniel Cabot Puts Down Roots

Copyright © 2022 by Cat Sebastian

All rights reserved. No part of this publication may be reproduced, stored or transmitted in any form or by any means, electronic, mechanical, photocopying, recording, scanning, or otherwise without written permission from the publisher. It is illegal to copy this book, post it to a website, or distribute it by any other means without permission.

First edition

This book was professionally typeset on Reedsy. Find out more at reedsy.com

Contents

Author's Note   v
Content Notes   vi

I   Part One

Chapter One	3
Chapter Two	6
Chapter Three	14
Chapter Four	27
Chapter Five	38
Chapter Six	47
Chapter Seven	60
Chapter Eight	75
Chapter Nine	87
Chapter Ten	96
Chapter Eleven	118
Chapter Twelve	134
Chapter Thirteen	149

II   Part Two

Chapter Fourteen	157
Chapter Fifteen	166
Chapter Sixteen	173

Chapter Seventeen	183
Chapter Eighteen	201
Chapter Nineteen	213
Chapter Twenty	223
Acknowledgments	233
About the Author	235
Also by Cat Sebastian	237

Author's Note

While this book is a part of the Cabot series, it's a standalone and you can enjoy it without having read the previous books. Daniel Cabot, one of this book's protagonists, previously appeared in *Tommy Cabot Was Here* as the titular character's twelve-year-old son.

This book takes place almost entirely in New York City's East Village. If you'd like to see a map of some places featured in the story, you can find one on my website at https://catsebastian.com/danielcabotmap/

Content Notes

One of the main characters in this book is neurodivergent and occasionally experiences some internalized ableism. He also was displaced from his home country during his childhood, and while this is never discussed in detail, it's a background fact of his life. There's some homophobia expressed by an antagonist.

I

Part One

May 1973
New York City

Chapter One

It was Mary's husband, home for the weekend, who started all the trouble.

They had reached the point in the evening where dinner had long since turned into drinks and drinks had turned into drinking. The four of them—Paul and Mary, Daniel and Alex—were lingering at a table in the back of the restaurant. They were all pretty comprehensively tipsy on frightening Hungarian brandy and it was going to take some time to even think about standing up. Alex's arm, warm and solid, was the only thing keeping Daniel from toppling off his chair.

"So how did you two meet?" Paul asked, cheerfully oblivious to the havoc he was about to wreak.

The difference between "how do you know one another" (a normal question to ask anyone) and "how did you meet" (which you only ask couples) might have been subtle enough to go over Alex's head, either because of the nuances of English, Alex's general indifference to social niceties, or the heroic quantity of pálinka they had drunk, but apparently it wasn't, and he visibly bristled. Daniel sighed, knowing they were all in for a night of it.

They'd been asked both versions of that question a dozen times before, usually by Daniel's friends, once by Daniel's mother, sometimes with a sort of cheerfully camp malice, but generally with undisguised curiosity as to how someone like Alex—beautiful, brilliant, sharp-edged Alex—came to be friends with someone as unremarkable as Daniel.

But Paul Chan was sincere. Earnest. A prince among men. Alex had described him as the least dickish surgeon he'd ever met.

The point was, Paul obviously was under the impression that Daniel and Alex were a *couple* couple.

Daniel sat up so Alex wouldn't have to make the choice to extract his arm. In the restaurant's dim lighting, Alex's cheekbones looked like they were cut from stone, his hair spun from white gold.

"We're not—" Alex began, but then petered out, clearly unsure of how to end that sentence without coming right out and saying *fucking* in the middle of a Hungarian restaurant.

Because what else could he possibly say? That they weren't together? They were nearly always together. That they weren't dating? Sure, fine, but here they both were on what was essentially a double date, and it was far from the first time that had happened. They celebrated holidays together. They had keys to one another's apartments. Alex called Daniel's mother on her birthday, and vice versa. Alex's nephew called Daniel *uncle*. It was Alex's phone number Daniel had written on the emergency card he kept in his wallet.

There was no way Alex could finish that sentence without lying unless he said they weren't fucking, which was true. It was true and it didn't change anything.

Across from them, Mary was clearly torn between kicking her husband under the table and settling in to enjoy the show. Daniel glared at her. She beamed at him. He had terrible taste in friends.

"He thought I was a junkie," Daniel supplied, because 1) that answered Paul's question, 2) it was a good story, one even Alex could make funny despite a total lack of comedic timing, and 3) bafflingly, Alex seemed to be under the impression that he came across as an asshole in this story, when the truth was the exact opposite.

And even when Daniel knew they were all going to have to endure Alex's pissy chilliness for the rest of the meal, he still wanted the world to know that Alex was, ultimately, kind of a sweetheart.

Daniel was an idiot, at least where Alex was concerned, and he had known it since the night they met.

Chapter Two

It was a year and a half ago, Alex minding his own damned business as he walked down Mercer Street after a middle-of-the-night house call on a newborn whose mother thought he had measles. Alex didn't do many house calls, but newborns had no business being outside in weather this cold, and it wasn't like Alex had anything better to do anyway. The baby, it turned out, didn't have measles, just standard newborn acne.

The sidewalks were slippery with ice and cluttered with garbage cans. It was late enough and Alex was tired enough that even though he only had a ten-minute walk to his apartment, he decided to hail a cab that was pulling up in front of one of the seedy nightclubs that peppered the neighborhood.

He crossed the street, lengthening his stride to catch the cab before it pulled away, when he realized that the loose crowd of people outside the club weren't waiting to get in, but were instead gathered around two men involved in the sort of incomprehensible shouting match that was either the prelude or accompaniment to a fistfight. Idiots. Even after nearly fifteen years in this country, he still couldn't understand Drunk American. He could perfectly comprehend three-year-olds and hold his own in any conversation about medicine, but was spared ever having to think about what drunk people said to one another, so he didn't have any complaints.

He turned toward the cab, but was shouldered aside by someone who was hauling one of the drunks away from the fight. The man had been shoved into the cab and the cab had pulled away from the curb before Alex could properly realize what had happened.

"Sorry about that. It figures he'd be a cab-stealer on top of everything else."

Alex turned to see a man with a bloody lip. A kid, really, not that much older than some of Alex's patients. Skinny, messy dark hair, pale skin, no coat. Holding one of his hands at an odd angle. Blood on his knuckles visible even in the flickering streetlight. Alex sighed.

"He was twice your size," Alex said, in case this kid didn't know he was an idiot.

"Didn't have much of a choice."

"Really," Alex asked, flat. "No choice."

"He called me some names." The kid shrugged. "Made some assumptions about the, uh, type of people I fuck and what I like to do with them."

Alex narrowed his eyes. "Fighting words," he said, testing the waters. If this kid thought being called queer was horrible enough to warrant punching someone in the face, well—Alex would still check out that injured hand, but he wouldn't like it.

The kid shrugged again. "I mean, he wasn't wrong. At least some of the time. Sixty percent, maybe? Honestly, it was more the way he said it. Like, you could tell it wasn't a compliment."

And fuck this guy, because that almost made Alex laugh. "Yeah, it usually isn't." He swallowed and added "unfortunately," in case the kid needed to know he was safe.

"It is if you have the right friends."

Alex had to concede the point. "Let me see your hand." The kid obediently held out his right hand. His knuckles were scuffed up—Alex found that he was glad the kid got in at least one hard punch—but it was his little finger that got Alex's attention. It was too soon for there to be much swelling, but he didn't think it was his imagination that the base of the finger felt a little hot. Gently, he pressed down on the fifth metacarpal, and the kid made a strangled sound.

"Fracture," Alex said. "You need X-rays and a splint."

"Yeah, no."

Alex looked carefully at the kid. Way too skinny, pale in a way that wasn't just from the ugly streetlight, not nearly enough clothes. Alex had lived in this neighborhood long enough to know what he was looking at. The junkies in this part of the city tended to be older, usually with dog tags, a beard, missing teeth. Over in Chelsea by the piers, though, near where Alex did his residency, they were younger, young enough to have been kicked out of their homes for being queer or to have run away before they could get kicked out, beating their parents to the punch—a stupid American idiom that made him wince in this context. A few blocks north you had the artist junkies, but they usually had addresses and bank accounts. There was a whole geography of heroin addiction that Alex didn't think he'd understand if he hadn't seen the pattern settle in over the city in the past ten years.

This guy wasn't the youngest addict Alex had seen, not even the youngest he'd seen with a broken hand. There was no way he would willingly go to a hospital; Alex was his best shot. He felt himself shift into doctor mode, and it was as much a relief as it always was. "What's your name?"

"Daniel."

"Okay, Daniel, I'm Alex. I'm a doctor. If I take you to my clinic, I can splint your finger. Would that be all right?"

"No." Not even any hesitation there, but not any attitude either, just a straightforward, factual *no*.

Alex didn't know whether to be annoyed that the kid wouldn't listen or relieved that he had enough self-preservation not to go off with a total stranger. "Okay, then let's get you some dinner." That, at least, was something Alex could do, and it looked like it had been a good long while since Daniel had anything to eat.

Daniel looked at him for a long minute, measured and skeptical. "All right," he said. "The diner on Lafayette is probably still open."

Alex could have told him that as far as he knew, that diner never closed. He and Mary used to practically live there during finals, both their family apartments too noisy and crowded to do much studying, libraries annoyingly closed overnight.

He kept a careful distance as they walked the few blocks to Lafayette.

* * *

Under the fluorescent lights of the diner, Alex immediately saw that he'd gotten the kid's age wrong. Or, rather, he saw that *kid* wasn't accurate in the first place. Daniel had to be twenty, probably more, but he had the sort of baby face that made judging these things difficult. He was old enough to have been drafted, which made everything else make sense. Mary's younger brother was barely twenty-two and Alex could only hope someone occasionally bought him dinner and made sure he was warm for at least part of the night.

The waitress brought ice and a towel and Daniel meekly submitted to letting Alex construct a primitive ice pack for his hand. The fracture didn't seem displaced, so if it was splinted and rested, it should heal fine. He wondered if there was anything in the kitchen he could use as a splint.

Daniel ordered a hamburger and Alex ordered—well, Alex ordered too much, thinking that he could probably convince Daniel to take the leftovers home with him, for whatever definition of home the kid had.

"Will you be needing anything else?" the waitress asked, giving Alex an unimpressed look after covering the table with fries, hashbrowns, pancakes, two plates of bacon, and a patty melt. He didn't know if the look was for ordering a wasteful amount of food, for bringing a junkie in, or for some other infraction he didn't even realize he'd committed.

"Ah, fuck," Daniel said when he tried to bring the burger to his mouth with what was probably his nondominant hand. A pickle and some onion rings fell onto the plate.

Alex pulled the plate across the table and cut the burger into bite-sized pieces, then slid it toward Daniel.

"Thanks." Daniel gave him an odd look but he ate his burger, so Alex wasn't going to let it bother him.

"What were you doing at that bar?" Alex asked, even though it didn't really matter. But people who weren't Mary hated eating in silence, and honestly, Mary did too, but she was good at filling up dead air with one-sided chatter. Besides, conversation was his best tactic for keeping Daniel at the table long enough to eat his fill.

"I was there for suicide," Daniel said.

Alex nearly choked on his pancakes. "You were what?" he asked when he got his breath back. He supposed getting attacked by men built like linebackers was one way to get the job done, but now Alex didn't know what to do. He couldn't dump the kid back on the street if he was only going to—

Daniel laughed, loud and uninhibited, showing all his teeth. Which—he had all his teeth. Huh. "They're a band. Suicide."

A tasteless name for what was no doubt a tasteless band, but it was still a relief. "Are they any good?" Again he was just filling the air, keeping Daniel talking and eating. Obviously, Daniel liked this band or he wouldn't have gone to see them.

"Eh," Daniel said, making a wavering gesture with his good hand and scrunching up his nose. "Jury's still out."

Well, okay then. "What do you like?" he asked, the same question he asked feverish toddlers and snippy twelve-year-olds and any other kid he wanted to draw out or distract, but probably a weird thing to ask an adult. Daniel didn't seem to notice, just embarked on the kind of monologue Alex was used to hearing, except instead of rambling about dinosaurs or American football, Daniel talked about music. Alex only understood about one word in ten. Same rate as for dinosaurs and football, actually.

Half Daniel's burger was uneaten and he was pushing the remnants around with his fork, which Alex recognized from eating with his nephew as a sign that the meal was done.

"Do you have anywhere to sleep?" Alex asked.

Something strange happened to Daniel's face, something Alex didn't bother trying to interpret. "Yes."

"Somewhere indoors?"

"Yes."

"Good." Alex paid, then managed to convince Daniel to take the leftovers by shoving the paper sack into his good arm and refusing to take no for an answer.

"My clinic is at the corner of First and First," Alex said when they stepped outside. "We open at nine, if you want me to splint your finger. Otherwise, keep it immobile and protected."

"What would you have done if I told you I didn't have anywhere to sleep?"

Alex didn't see what this had to do with splints. "I'd have given you a subway token, two dollars, and directions to the YMCA," he said, because that was the truth and it was neither more nor less than what he'd done for other people in Daniel's situation.

"You weren't trying to pick me up, then."

Alex might have been offended that Daniel thought he was the kind of person who picked up men who were down on their luck, maybe too down on their luck to refuse. But Daniel didn't know him, and maybe it was a fair assumption. Maybe he was used to that sort of thing. Alex didn't like to think about it.

"No," Alex said. "I do not pick up men by offering first aid."

"Yeah, I doubt you have to go to that kind of trouble." There was no leer to accompany those words, no wink, no hint that it was anything there other than a frank statement of fact, which—well, he was right. Alex didn't have to go to much trouble, which was good because otherwise he'd be basically celibate. Mary told him all the time that it was a good thing he could get by on his looks. She wasn't wrong.

"Thanks for everything," Daniel said, and headed east. Alex needed to go east too, but he didn't want Daniel to think he was being followed, so he headed north. He would turn crosstown later, even though this route would mean longer in the freezing cold. He looked over his shoulder and saw Daniel looking back. Daniel waved with his right hand, then winced.

"Keep it immobilized!" Alex shouted, too loud for the hour,

for the lack of traffic.

Daniel turned back around, and so did Alex, and that, he thought, was that.

Alex wasn't expecting it when Daniel showed up at the clinic two days later with a neatly splinted hand, insisting on taking Alex out to dinner to thank him. He wasn't expecting that dinner to last so long that waiters began pointedly stacking chairs and wiping down nearby tables.

For the first few months, he waited for Daniel to find something better to do, to get tired of whatever it was he saw in Alex, because that was what inevitably happened. It didn't, though, not even when Alex snapped at him for springing both his parents on Alex without warning, not even when Alex got tired and cranky and his weak grasp of the social graces slipped away entirely.

Being friends with Daniel was effortless in a way nothing had ever been for Alex. He'd never made a friend before—Mary didn't count, because she was the one who'd made him a friend, and all he had to do was go along with it.

But Daniel was a friend, a real friend, something so rare and good that there was no use thinking about anything else he could have been.

And so Alex very nearly didn't.

Chapter Three

"Sorry you got accused of being my boyfriend," Daniel said when they stepped outside the Hungarian restaurant.

Alex huffed, unamused. If he were anyone else, the fact that his blood was currently mostly composed of fruit brandy might have made him more tolerant, less irritable, but instead the alcohol made him unable to put the brakes on his annoyance.

"Paul was only trying to be supportive," Daniel added.

Paul had known about Alex being gay from the second semester of medical school, about the time it looked like Mary would be keeping this boyfriend around. Alex would concede that he didn't pick up on a lot of nuance, but he might have guessed that Paul was supportive around the time that Paul looked up from the newspaper the day after the Stonewall riots and said, "I support gay rights, in case you were wondering," and Alex responded with, "Okay," and Mary said, "Wow, so mushy, gross."

It wasn't Paul's fault. It probably wasn't even Mary's. It was just—he and Daniel weren't a couple, so the assumption rubbed him the wrong way. That was all. He didn't like the idea of people thinking about him in the first place, and liked it even less when what they were wrong in their assumptions. He shouldn't have to explain it. He shouldn't have to justify his irritation, not even to himself. It didn't have anything to do with how he preferred not to think about Daniel in that way and resented being forced to.

What was he supposed to have told Paul? "We're just friends?" That would have communicated the point Paul presumably was interested in but still manage to be dishonest, because Alex had, for what it was worth, had sex with a lot of people but he had only ever had two friends, and there had never been any overlap there. There was no "just" where friends were concerned, not for Alex.

"I like for my private life to be private," he snapped at Daniel now.

"I know," Daniel said, too nice for someone who was being unfairly snapped at. "Is this the kind of night where you're mean to me while we watch TV at your apartment or do you need to disappear for a few days?"

That only made Alex crankier, because he didn't want to be mean to Daniel, which was why he sometimes stayed away when he was in a pissy mood. But sometimes there wasn't an alternative. If he looked at Daniel, he'd see the jagged edges between what they were to one another and what he sometimes—only sometimes, mind you, in his more pathetic moments—wanted them to be.

He was incredibly good at not thinking about that. Honestly, one of his strengths was not thinking about things that wouldn't do anyone any good to think about. He got through medical school by not thinking about anything but medical school; he got through that strange, lost year between Lviv and New York by not thinking about anything at all; he would get through this by not thinking of Daniel as anything other than a friend, but right then he couldn't do that if Daniel was anywhere nearby.

"The second thing," Alex gritted out, annoyed, but also grateful that Daniel didn't make him ask for it.

"I'll see you Monday, then," Daniel said easily. Too fucking easily. The way he cheerfully accepted Alex's shittiest moods, not taking them personally even when they *were* sort of personal, was just one of the things Alex loved about him and therefore not something he could deal with right now.

Alex turned toward his apartment without saying good night.

"Good night," he heard Daniel call.

Oh, for fuck's sake.

"Good night," he called back.

"See you Monday!"

"See you Monday, Daniel."

* * *

Daniel Cabot didn't believe in love at first sight. He refused to be the type of person who believed in love at first sight, and after all, he didn't really love Alex from the moment they met or anything. It was maybe half an hour later, when Alex cut up his burger. And it probably wasn't even love, anyway, just some other kind of overwhelming fondness coupled with a conviction that he had to keep Alex in his life.

Besides, that feeling, whatever it was, might have dissipated if Daniel hadn't stopped by Alex's office two days later and seen Alex signing a little girl's cast, then heard him speaking softly to her mother in a language Daniel couldn't understand. That was probably when his fate was sealed.

No, that wasn't true either. Daniel could have stayed away, especially after it was clear that Alex didn't want him, not in that way. But Daniel didn't stay away, and now he couldn't, and he didn't even want to.

Whatever it was, it had long since faded into a background fact of his life, like the clang of his radiators or the salsa music his upstairs neighbors played almost constantly—he barely even noticed it, and even when he did notice, he didn't need to do anything about it. It was pleasant, almost, a warm undercurrent to the most solid friendship of his life.

He didn't even care that Alex didn't want to see him for two days. Mostly.

"I'm not going to tell you that he treats you like shit," Lauren said, emptying the dregs of a bottle of chianti into Daniel's glass. After leaving Alex, Daniel had gotten on the subway and shown up unannounced at Lauren and Jacob's apartment.

"You're just going to imply it," Daniel said. It had been a mistake to come here, had been an even bigger mistake to tell them about Alex getting pissy at dinner.

"I don't think he treats you badly," Jacob said, sounding pretty dubious about it.

"Shouldn't have introduced you," Daniel mumbled into his wine glass.

Both Lauren and Jacob sent him identical looks that said *obviously*. He wanted his friends to get along. Was that so wrong? If he liked a person, then other people he liked should feel the same, right? Like a transitive property of friendship or something. When he had tried to explain this, Alex had sighed and said that only someone as bad at math as Daniel would think this made any sense.

It had been a disaster of an evening when Daniel first brought

Alex to meet Lauren and Jacob, Alex glaring every time Jacob's arm slipped along the back of Daniel's chair, his gaze practically burning holes into the side of Lauren's head when she leaned in to kiss Daniel goodbye. Daniel had known Alex for three months at that point, long enough to know he would be keeping Alex, but not well enough to understand that Alex needed to be introduced to people carefully, in small, isolated doses, in quiet settings, and with his friends warned beforehand that Alex was shy.

On the subway platform on the way home that awful night, Alex had stared at the dirty tile wall across the tracks. "Which of them are you fucking? I couldn't tell."

"Both," Daniel had said immediately, startled into it. Not that he would have lied, but he might have managed to delicately lead up to the truth if he had known the question was coming. He ought to have expected unvarnished honesty from Alex by then. "It's pretty casual, though."

"They're married," Alex said, not bothering to conceal his distaste.

"Well, it isn't casual for them, obviously. Not with one another, I mean."

Alex blinked. "And they both know?"

Daniel had frowned, confused. "They're both—I sleep with both of them. Look, it might not be an arrangement that you like, but it suits them and it suits me." Sometimes they wanted a third, and sometimes Daniel wanted to have sex that wasn't exactly casual but also wasn't complicated. They all knew where they stood: Jake and Lauren had been in love with one another since college and neither of them were in love with Daniel, or he with them, and that suited all three of them. This particular arrangement wouldn't be forever, but it was nice for now.

"You sleep with them both together. At the same time."

"Yep. Wait. Did you think I was having an affair? Two affairs?" Daniel had started laughing, which must have done something to unwind Alex a little bit, because his mouth tipped up a bit. "I'm so insulted," Daniel sputtered.

"I was trying not to sound judgmental!"

"You really, really failed."

After that night, Daniel had thought that the worst was over and Alex could get to know Daniel's closest friends, but no, Alex acted like a hissy cat the second time too. By the fourth time, he settled into something mildly peeved, and by the time a year had passed, they were almost friends. A few weeks earlier, Alex gave Lauren a book for her birthday and Daniel managed not to look shocked.

But throughout that time, Alex had never declined an invitation to see them; he knew that Daniel believed in the spurious transitive property of friendship, and so he kept trying.

"He doesn't treat me badly," Daniel said. "It's just that sometimes he needs to take some time off."

"Time off from being your friend," Lauren said, skeptical.

"No, time off from—I don't know. He doesn't stop being my friend. Don't be like that." Sometimes reality was just too much and Alex needed to spend a few days prescribing antibiotics and weighing babies, because those things made sense, those things were predictable, measurable, finite. But Daniel didn't know how to explain that without giving away more than Alex might want him to.

Lauren and Jacob shared a look, a secret married people look that made Daniel feel about fourteen. "Have you thought that maybe he wants more from you?" Lauren asked.

"It's not that," Daniel mumbled. He wished it were, but it wasn't, and he was fine.

"He's jealous of us," Lauren said. "Have you dated anyone since you met?"

Daniel glared at them, or at least he tried to. He had it on good authority (his mom, laughing in his face) that his glare was pretty nonthreatening. The truth was that he had had less than a handful of exclusive lovers in his life. Typically, he made friends, he had sex with them, he had sex with his new friends' friends, and so forth. It was all very...friendly. There wasn't anything serious about it. He'd dated a few girls in college, but nobody he really wanted to stay with. Lauren and Jacob knew all this because they had been around for most of it, and they probably thought they were making some big point.

He was glad that Jacob and Lauren were happy together, but that wasn't what he wanted for himself. He liked going home to his shitty apartment at the end of the day and knowing that nobody would talk to him until he wanted to talk. He liked having time to spend with friends and the option to lose an entire weekend to puttering in the garden or dicking around on an article without having to think of anyone or anything else. This probably made him a dirtbag, but honestly, he was a happy dirtbag. He couldn't see how settling down with anyone would improve that.

And then there was Alex—the fact of him, the way Daniel shaped his days around a space that Alex might sometimes occupy, the predictable rhythm of Alex's routine the heartbeat of Daniel's life. They weren't a couple, but they were a pair, and Daniel couldn't imagine dating someone when he had Alex. He wasn't particularly impressed with monogamy as a concept, but having Alex made the idea of dating someone feel redundant. The fact that Alex didn't feel the same way about him didn't really enter into the equation. Whatever Alex felt was Alex's business, and—more importantly—it was enough.

The fact was that Daniel liked his life. He was twenty-six and he liked his life. And that was no small thing—there was no getting away from the fact that thousands of people his exact age weren't as lucky, and had been sent off to fight a war almost nobody thought was a good idea, while Daniel had spent a year at a desk in Panama, brushing up on his high school Spanish, filing papers, and reading novels. And if that—the near miss of it all, the there-but-for-the-grace-of-God feeling he got every day—left him a little shattered, a little at sea, that was nothing.

But people who were happily in love wanted to see romance everywhere they looked. Lauren and Jacob weren't going to rest until everyone they knew was paired off (or tripled off, or whatever). "Are you guys just trying to make me date someone so you'll stop having to fuck me?" Daniel grumbled.

"Yeah, Dan, that's our master plan," Jacob said, rolling his eyes. "Because fucking you is such a hardship."

And then one of them started in on his belt, thank God, so they could finally stop having this conversation.

* * *

When Alex turned his key in the lock of his apartment door, he could hear the phone ringing inside. It was past ten, and the only person who'd be calling him at that hour was the clinic's answering service.

He tried not to sound too disappointed when he heard Mary's voice on the line.

"Shouldn't you be spending time with your husband?" Paul was in his last year of surgical residency at a hospital in Philadelphia, and they were making do with odd weekends and holidays until he moved back to the city in the fall.

"We already did that and now he's asleep," she said.

Alex sighed. He hadn't meant it as a euphemism and she knew he hadn't, but that wasn't going to stop her. He knew from experience that nothing ever would.

"It's late," he pointed out.

"I need to talk to you about what happened at dinner."

Alex winced. He'd hoped that only Daniel had noticed his mood, but of course it hadn't escaped Mary, either. "Will you apologize to Paul for me?" he said automatically.

"It's not that. He feels bad. I should have explained to him ages ago that you two aren't officially a couple."

"What do you mean, officially."

"I get that you two are going at your own pace, and that's—"

"There's no pace! There's—we're friends. That's—Mary, come on, you know this."

Mary was silent for a moment, but he could hear her fiddling with the phone cord. "Why, though?"

"Why?"

"Why aren't you together?"

He could get Mary off his back by saying he wasn't interested in Daniel, which was partly true. He had never tried to date anyone, and had planned to live out the rest of his years without bothering to learn how. He certainly didn't want to try and then fail with someone as important as Daniel. "How is that even a question?" he asked. "Why are any two random people not together?"

Mary ignored this, as she ignored all Alex's clumsy attempts at dishonesty. "He touches you," she said.

Alex felt his face heat and was glad that Mary couldn't see it, even though she probably somehow knew anyway. "He's a touchy person."

"You flinch when your mother hugs you. You'd probably flinch if I hugged you."

Alex and Mary met when they were fifteen, on the subway up to the Bronx for high school. She sat next to him, and then sat there the following day and the day after that, predictable and quiet. The memory of how quiet she was jarred him now. She must have been lying in wait.

They had most of the same classes and did their homework together on the train back to Manhattan or later at the library. His spoken English was still mediocre then, even though his reading and writing must have been decent enough to get him into Bronx Science. But Mary was a native speaker—she spoke Cantonese at home but had been born in New York—and he started to go to her whenever he needed a new idiom explained or hadn't caught a teacher's rapid-fire instructions. She patiently explained it all to him and then started to talk about everything else. She didn't seem to need much in the way of contribution from him, so he just let her conversation wash over him.

By the end of tenth grade, his English was as good as it was ever going to get, but he still didn't understand everything. Sometimes he couldn't understand why a person said a certain thing, or acted a certain way. Usually Mary could make sense of it, and she always just treated it as another kind of translation.

The point was, Mary knew him. She knew his preferences and his peculiarities, and she knew how he fit—or, rather, didn't—into the world.

"I'd hug you," he grumbled.

"I'd never ask you to."

It wasn't that Alex hated being touched; he just always suspected that his response was slightly wrong—too stiff, a second too late, too obviously lacking in affection. He didn't care for being surprised, either, and so many touches seemed to come out of the blue.

But when a patient wanted to hug him, he got down to their level and hugged them back. It was straightforward. They were happy to see him, or glad to have their stitches out, or sad that they didn't get to keep their tonsils in a creepy little jar, and they wanted a hug, so that's what they got. He didn't really understand why, say, his mother wanted to hug him when they were both stiff and awkward the entire time, then relieved to sit on opposite ends of the couch and revert to conversation about antacids or income tax.

When his nephew was interested, Alex hugged him or held him in his lap for a story. He held his baby niece whenever he had a chance. Again, it was straightforward. Babies wanted to be held; some children liked to be physically close to the people they loved.

Daniel, though—maybe it was because Alex had first thought of him as a patient. Maybe that slotted Daniel into the category of person Alex didn't mind being touched by, even though he was very much aware now that Daniel was an adult and not his patient. Maybe it was because Daniel needed touch the way plants needed sunlight. Sometimes when they were watching television, Daniel would creep steadily closer, giving Alex plenty of time to get used to the idea, until Alex—amused, despite himself—gave in, wrapping an arm around Daniel, receiving Daniel's head against his shoulder. Daniel always seemed so pleased by it that Alex was never left wondering whether he was doing it right.

It wasn't sexual with Daniel. He was sure of that. Sex was another context where Alex was okay with touching, obviously, but he was pretty utilitarian about sex.

"You treat it like something that needs to be done, like going to the barber," Daniel had said after the third or fourth time they had gone out to a bar together with the explicit purpose of finding people to have sex with. "Only, a sexy barber."

"I'm not listening to anything you say about barbers," Alex had responded, eyeing Daniel's increasingly chaotic mop of hair.

"You just stand there, looking beautiful and annoyed, until someone acceptable comes up to you, and then you go off with him. The next day you're scowling maybe fifteen percent less."

"I'm not listening to anything you say about percentages, either."

"I wonder if I'm pretty enough to get away with using scowling as a pick-up method," Daniel mused. "I doubt it."

"Oh, for fuck's sake." Alex had put a hand over Daniel's mouth until Daniel tried to bite him.

"Alex," Mary said, calling him back to the present. "You need to talk to Daniel."

"I talk to him almost every day."

She didn't sigh, but he heard her *not* sigh. "He looked upset at dinner."

"He knew I was going to be difficult later on. Of course he was upset."

"Have you considered not being difficult? Or, I don't know, slightly less difficult? Just with Daniel, maybe?"

Alex didn't know how to respond to that. He didn't set out

to make life hard for the people around him, for the people he cared for enough to *let* be around him. Mary knew all that.

"Sorry," Mary said. "I shouldn't have said that."

"No, you're right. I'm not a very good friend."

"That's not what I meant."

It might not have been what she meant, but it was true anyway.

Chapter Four

When Daniel got back to America after his useless stint in the Army, he went to New York because his mother was there, not that he'd ever admit that to her. He brought two suitcases of clothes, one crate of records, and a record player to an apartment that already contained a bed and a chair, and which he could afford even if his employment prospects turned out to be worse than he expected.

He then proceeded to spend six months doing precisely fuck all, going to shows and listening to the new-sounding music that had appeared out of nowhere, music that felt as jagged and reckless as he did, bitter and exuberant in equal parts. He drank too much, punched a couple of dickheads, and—almost as an afterthought—wrote some music reviews which the *Village Voice* inexplicably paid him money for.

But then he met Alex—hard-working, ambitious, kind, generous Alex, who had just opened a sliding-scale pediatrics clinic right between the upper reaches of Chinatown and the part of the East Village where Ukrainian immigrants clustered. Alex spoke Ukrainian and Russian; Mary spoke Cantonese and Mandarin; they both spoke fluent English and enough Spanish to get by.

Daniel had felt like a slob and a layabout in comparison, and even more so when he thought about how little effort it would take for him to get a job doing something Officially Worthwhile: nothing more than a couple of phone calls to his father, a cousin, maybe an old classmate.

Instead, he started breaking up the ground in the empty lot next to his apartment building where a couple of old tenements had burned down years earlier.

At the time, what he knew about gardening could have fit on a postage stamp, but he could dig a hole. He could dig a hole, and he could deal with cops staring at him, and that made him the man for the job.

It had been his neighbors' idea.

"Do we know who owns that lot?" Daniel had asked.

"Do we care? Does he care? He wants to build something there, he can be my guest," Blanca Martinez had said in a way that made *be my guest* sound like a string of profanities. "But until then, we can use the space."

Beside her, Miriam Epstein had nodded, passing Daniel a joint. "It gets good light."

And so Daniel had set about clearing the lot, hauling away bricks and rocks in a wheelbarrow that appeared one morning and whose origin he wasn't looking into too closely. He piled them in a corner of the space, thinking they could later on be used to divide garden beds. He was pretty sure that was how garden beds worked, at least. Gardening was very much not on the curriculum at the kind of schools he attended.

He spent that first winter and into the spring clearing away rubble and doing his best to make sure the space was safe: no rusty nails, no jagged glass. Alex, mutely horrified, had stitched his hand up twice and insisted on tetanus shots. After the second time, Daniel bought sturdier work gloves, and Blanca, whether out of some sense of fair trade or simply pity, had come over to caulk Daniel's windows, which really had done wonders for the mold situation.

That first spring, some friends of Blanca's arrived with a truckload of dirt, and then everybody had stood around with bottles of beer, admiring the empty lot.

It still hadn't looked like much of a garden. It looked exactly like what it was: an empty lot that someone had dumped a truckload of dirt into.

"You have to see the potential," Miriam said. "All gardens start with bare dirt."

This was obviously true, but most gardens likely didn't start with felony trespass and tetanus shots.

But then a couple of kids from across the street wandered over to play in the dirt pile, and that's when it hit Daniel—a truckload of dirt in a lot that was devoid of broken glass was an improvement. If they managed to get anything at all to grow here, that would be a bonus. The point wasn't to make the prettiest garden—the point was to reclaim this patch of earth for the neighborhood, to mark it out as something that hadn't been abandoned.

"You did good work, rich boy," Blanca said.

Daniel rolled his eyes at this, but there was no use denying it. There was no imaginable future in which Daniel wouldn't have a roof over his head and food on his plate.

Blanca had made it clear that this was a community garden, not Daniel's pet project to assuage his bourgeois guilt, and that if he needed to spend money to feel better about his lot in life, he could chip in for apartment 2B's late rent and not spend it on begonias. And so instead, Daniel got a library card and took out books about gardening. He dug holes. He hooked up a hose to a water line he was pretty sure nobody was paying for, and he hoped nobody noticed. One of the grandfathers from across the street pointed at places in the ground and told Daniel in a Spanish he hardly recognized what to plant there.

Now, a year after that first truckload of dirt, it really did look like a garden, if not an especially nice one.

If it hadn't been for the garden, Daniel probably would have moved when his lease was up. The building was crumbling and the landlord was distinctly uninterested in doing anything about it. He could have afforded to move to a better neighborhood, even marginally better, like what he might find a few blocks further west on East 6th Street, closer to Alex's apartment. But now he had gotten to know his neighbors and he liked knowing who to say hello to as he passed them on the sidewalk or on the stairs.

Daniel's parents had separated when he was twelve, and since then he had always split his time between their homes, usually with boarding school or college serving as yet another temporary home. This apartment, however awful, marked the first time he'd had one single place to call home. The garden, however humble, might be the first thing he had ever accomplished with his own hands.

And at the end of every day, Daniel was exhausted, tired enough that all he knew for sure was that the sun was shining and the seedlings were, if not thriving, then not dying either.

* * *

On Monday night Daniel showed up at Alex's apartment with

a brown paper bag of groceries, both he and it half soaked in rain.

It wasn't the first time—Daniel didn't have a stove in his horrible little apartment, just a hot plate he plugged in over Alex's protests that it was a fire hazard—so he sometimes made dinner at Alex's. He wasn't a good cook, but neither was Alex, and the meals Daniel semi-competently prepared were different from the meals Alex semi-competently prepared, so at least they had variety on their side.

But when he unpacked the groceries, there was only a pound of butter, a box of cake mix, and some eggs, all sitting confusingly on Alex's counter.

"Why are you making cake?" It wasn't either of their birthdays, not that they were in the habit of making cake for the birthdays they spent together. Alex couldn't think of any situation that would call for boxed cake mix, anyway. There was a good Ukrainian bakery that Daniel would have had to walk past in order to get here and Veniero's was only a few blocks out of the way.

"It's brownies, actually," Daniel said, which didn't really explain anything.

Brownies were objectively disgusting. Perhaps Alex was being punished with gross American pastry. Daniel didn't usually hold Alex's pissy moods against him, and Alex didn't know why it even occurred to him that this time might be different—only that for some reason it felt different to Alex.

He watched Daniel dump the contents of the box and the rest of the ingredients into a bowl with an alarming lack of precision—half that egg wound up in the sink—then stirred it all with a fork. Alex was pretty sure you weren't supposed to use a fork. There was a whisk in the top drawer, but Daniel already knew this.

Alex noticed that Daniel hadn't preheated the oven, so he turned the dials until he heard the pilot light flare up.

"Thanks." Daniel poured the batter into a pan and slid the pan into the oven. The oven hadn't finished preheating, but Alex doubted that brownies were the kind of food that required accurate baking. They certainly didn't taste like it. "Try this." Daniel held up the fork he used to stir.

Alex turned his head away. "Raw eggs. And I don't like brownies even when they're cooked." Except—was he being rude? Maybe the brownies were a peace offering? A totally unnecessary one, because if anyone ought to be apologizing, it was Alex. "I'm sorry," he added.

"Not everybody likes brownies," Daniel said reasonably, speaking around the batter-covered fork that was already in his mouth.

"Not about that. About..." He trailed off, because part of the problem was that he wasn't entirely sure what to apologize for. He had already apologized for being testy the other day, but that didn't undo his meanness. It was just that he felt very conscious that most people wouldn't appreciate their friends effectively telling them to stay away for two days and then cheerfully come over to make brownies. Alex knew by now that Daniel wasn't going to stop being his friend, but sometimes he thought that Daniel shouldn't want to be.

Alex washed the bowl in silent atonement. Then he noticed that Daniel hadn't set the timer, so he fished the brownie box out of the garbage, checked the instructions, and set the timer for twenty-five minutes.

"Alex, we're fine. Just come sit down." Daniel was tucked against the arm of the sofa. He had a knack for making himself small.

"Did you eat dinner?" Alex asked.

"That's what the brownies are for."

Alex didn't bother pointing out that brownies weren't dinner, that brownies had never been dinner and they never would be, and that honestly, they shouldn't even be dessert. He just took a couple apples out of the refrigerator and sliced them the way his mother used to, arranged them on a plate with some cheddar cheese, and put the plate on the coffee table.

Daniel was watching a game show—not really watching it, but existing in the same room as a television that happened to be tuned in to a game show. Between that, and the brownies, and the way he was crumpled against the arm of the sofa, Alex knew something wasn't right.

"What's the matter?" Alex asked.

"Long day. Turns out you have to dig a really fucking deep hole to plant a tree."

"What kind of tree?"

"No idea. I'm just the muscle."

This was both the truth—Alex was sometimes all too aware of what had happened to Daniel's arms and shoulders since he started working on that garden—and an outright falsehood because Daniel had managed to accumulate a wealth of odd facts and trivia about plants, insects, and various fungi. If he didn't know what kind of tree it was, that was because Daniel's friend Blanca and her accomplices hadn't yet stolen it—excuse him, *liberated* it—from someone who didn't deserve nice plants.

"You'll feel better if you eat," Alex said. "I bet you haven't eaten since lunch."

"Might have had some crackers," Daniel mumbled. And since

Daniel seldom ate breakfast, this painted a pretty grim picture of the day. Daniel was twenty-six. He shouldn't have to be told to eat. But the embarrassing truth was that they both needed these reminders. Daniel often arrived at the clinic with an armload of Chinese takeout or a pizza, without which Alex might not remember to eat dinner—or he'd remember, but only after he got home and was too tired to make anything other than eggs and toast. Again.

Alex picked up the plate of fruit and cheese and put it in front of Daniel's face until Daniel took a few bites.

When the timer sounded, Alex got up, waving Daniel back to the sofa.

"You need to put it in the freezer," Daniel called when Alex took the pan out of the oven. "Otherwise it'll take forever to cool down."

This was probably terrible for the freezer and bad for the food inside it, but Daniel really needed to eat something and Alex was feeling obliging and remorseful, so he put the brownies in the freezer, setting aside a box of frozen broccoli and some foil-wrapped pierogi to make room. Tomorrow he would throw out any food that looked suspicious.

When Alex sat back down, Daniel began to do the thing where he somehow oozed across the sofa without actually moving a single body part in any discernible way. He was like a slime mold. Alex decided, for the sake of expediency, to cut to the chase. He held out his arm. "Come here."

Daniel wriggled over, tucking himself under Alex's arm, then giving a little sigh when he got himself settled. For some reason, Alex had to suppress the echo of that sigh; it wasn't as if he was even comfortable with Daniel's elbows poking his ribs or his hair constantly landing in Alex's mouth.

"Going out tonight?" Alex asked. Daniel often went out with friends after having dinner with Alex, either to hear a band or just to have drinks. Alex knew he was being fit into an odd free hour or two of Daniel's life, that for the space of dinner or lunch, Daniel made room for Alex.

"No," Daniel mumbled into the fabric of Alex's shirt. "Too tired."

Alex probably ought to make sure Daniel didn't fall asleep before he ate his brownies, that way he could leave before Alex had to go to bed.

Alex always hated sending Daniel home, probably because Daniel's apartment was horrible. The first time Alex visited, he nearly spun on his heel and left. It was two rooms, if you counted a bed-sized alcove as a room, which Daniel apparently did. There was a shower next to the kitchen sink—not a bathtub, which Alex had seen in some older apartments, but an actual shower stall of the sort you might find in a locker room. The floor was oddly spongy, and in the spring, sickly-looking mushrooms grew on the windowsill. The entire building held a permanent odor of marijuana smoke, only some of which could possibly be Daniel's, as even Daniel didn't smoke *that* much. It was located on a stretch of East Sixth where Alex once saw a car on fire, a part of Alphabet City where you could never get a cab. It was a ten-minute walk to the nearest subway station.

But Daniel said he liked it, which Alex supposed had to be true because Daniel could afford better. He had money, family money, which he only mentioned that one time Alex outright offered to pay first and last month's rent on a less shitty apartment.

Alex nudged Daniel's shoulder. "Come on. Your brownies will be frozen solid."

When Daniel got to his feet and stretched, Alex made sure not to look at the sliver of skin exposed when his shirt rode up, the hint of musculature that almost certainly hadn't been there a year and a half ago when Alex had mistaken him for a starving vagrant.

The brownies were indeed half frozen, capable of being sliced into neat squares instead of the usual semisolid blobs. Like this, they looked almost edible.

"I'm going to try one," Alex announced.

"Go for it," Daniel said, his mouth already full.

He chose one near the edge, because those looked least in danger of mushiness, and took a careful bite. It was cold and—yeah, the texture of brownies was never not going to be disturbing, but like this, it wasn't bad. It was like a cross between a candy bar and a cookie, both things he mostly liked but which had never needed to be crossbred.

"Are you going to survive it?" Daniel asked.

"It was all right."

Daniel looked inordinately pleased.

"You should stay," Alex said when they were settled back on the sofa. "It's still raining. You'll never get a cab." He was never getting a cab anyway, not to bring him to his awful neighborhood, but Alex was feeling too nice to mention that. The urge to keep Daniel out of the rain was objectively ridiculous; Alex had four umbrellas and could lend him one. He was a grown adult who could endure getting wet on what was only a short walk. And yet Alex really did not want Daniel to leave.

"Really?" Daniel asked, but it wasn't a real question—he knew Alex didn't offer things without meaning it. That, Alex suspected, was why they worked as friends: Alex was blunt and fundamentally disinterested in polite dishonesty, and Daniel was unfailingly truthful and had a robust enough ego that he wasn't bothered by what other people considered Alex's rudeness. If either of them had expected anything other than honesty, it would have been a disaster.

He'd never offered for Daniel to stay the night before, though. But tonight—well, he still felt a little guilty, even though Daniel obviously had moved on. He wanted to make it better, which wasn't rational, because Daniel said it was fine. And offering his sofa for the night wouldn't actually make anything better, but it kept Daniel out of the rain, and that was something, at least.

He looked at the pleased little smile on Daniel's face as he helped himself to another brownie, and realized the truth of the situation. He'd offered to let Daniel spend the night because he knew it would make Daniel happy, and that had been reason enough.

Chapter Five

Somehow, Daniel had never noticed that Alex's sofa was the loudest piece of furniture in the history of squeaky springs. Despite not being especially tall, he kept needing to shift to make room for his legs, and every time he moved, the sofa let out a protest that had to wake Alex as well as the rest of the building and possibly the residents of the nearest cemetery.

He made an effort to lie perfectly still, but that only made him more desperate to roll over. Was he always this fidgety and hadn't noticed until now? Why was he suddenly incapable of just shutting his eyes and going the fuck to sleep? He had nearly fallen asleep six times while they were watching that stupid game show, so what the fuck, Daniel?

"There's room in my bed," said Alex from the doorway to his bedroom. "Either get in or I'll have to kill you." His voice had the faint traces of an accent that only cropped up when he was very tired.

Daniel grabbed the pillow he was using and followed Alex into his room.

"Good night," Daniel said when he was settled on Alex's bed, the sheets cool and crisp beneath him, Alex's blanket soft and smelling like fabric softener on top of him.

"Good night. Now go to sleep," Alex mumbled.

It was only midnight. Maybe that's why Daniel wasn't sleeping. He usually didn't fall asleep until past two, since part of his job was to hear live music and that didn't tend to happen during business hours. But today he was ragged from gardening, and that tended to knock him out as soon as his head hit the pillow.

Now, though, he was uncomfortably aware of not being in his own bed. Not that he was any kind of stranger to sleeping in other people's beds, to be fair. But the sounds rising up from the street were subtly different here than they were at his own apartment. They were the same nighttime sounds as you'd find anywhere in the city—sirens, the occasional car horn, a dog barking, doors opening and shutting, trash cans being rattled by God knew what—but arranged a little differently, a subtly altered composition. That shouldn't be enough to keep him awake, let alone hold his attention.

Daniel had spent countless hours in this apartment and never had it felt so strange.

It was just—there was Alex, not even two feet away from him, wearing a T-shirt and pajama pants instead of being all buttoned up and smoothed down. In the streetlight that filtered through the curtains, his hair was nearly white. His shoulders rose and fell steadily enough that he had to be asleep. He was on his side, turned sensibly away from Daniel, which was really what Daniel ought to be doing instead of watching him.

You would think that it was Daniel who was new to sharing a bed. Which made him wonder—did Alex actually *sleep* with his lovers? Daniel didn't think so, would have thought he'd have heard about it. Maybe in the past, though, before Daniel knew him? As far as Daniel knew, Alex only had one-night stands, and it was hard to imagine him tolerating a stranger in his apartment longer than strictly necessary, or to voluntarily sleep anywhere besides his own bed.

Daniel had never considered himself jealous—it felt unenlightened, somehow, like he had some kind of dibs on another person—but felt a surge of hot jealousy toward anyone who had shared Alex's bed, literally or figuratively. This was probably just a sign that he was exhausted.

It was probably also a sign that he ought to have gone home to his own bed instead of letting ideas get into his head. This was dangerous, too close to the real thing. He had made his peace—sort of—with Alex not being interested in him. Alex got spooked at the mere implication that they were a couple.

But Alex also, as a matter of routine, cuddled Daniel and kissed the top of his head when he thought Daniel was asleep on his shoulder. He didn't do that with anyone else, of that Daniel was sure. That had to count for something, but Daniel didn't know what and hadn't known for over a year.

He made himself roll over to face the wall.

* * *

It was Alex's fault. He wasn't used to sharing a bed, didn't know that he'd unconsciously reach for the nearest warm body, certainly didn't know that Daniel wouldn't react by immediately moving away. Didn't know that *he* wouldn't react by moving away either.

When he woke up, it was with his chest flush against the warmth of Daniel's back, an arm dropped heavily over Daniel's side, his nose buried in the curls at the nape of Daniel's neck.

CHAPTER FIVE

His alarm hadn't gone off yet, and he was in a sleepy state of confusion when somehow it made sense that he was smelling Daniel's shampoo, that for some reason they were—he was afraid there was no other word than *cuddling*—in his bed rather than on the sofa watching television. Even his half hard cock pressing against the curve of Daniel's ass didn't seem out of place. Before even knowing he was awake, he had shifted, liked it, done it again.

As soon as he realized what he was doing, he went still, horrified, frozen in place. Daniel was probably still asleep, probably wouldn't wake up for another three hours. All Alex had to do was extricate his arm and ease backwards and it would be like this never happened.

But then Daniel moved, and if Alex didn't know better, he'd have thought Daniel was pushing his hips back against Alex.

"You can, you know," Daniel said, his voice rough from sleep.

For a minute, all Alex knew was visceral horror that Daniel had been awake for that. And then—

"I—what?" Alex rolled onto his back.

"You can, you know. If you want." Daniel waved an idle hand in the air.

Alex got out of bed. "I *can*? If I *want*?"

"It doesn't have to be—I mean, I'm here, you're—" He rolled to face Alex and gestured mortifyingly in the vicinity of Alex's groin. "It doesn't have to be a big deal."

For Christ's sake, Alex was no stranger to sex not being a big deal, was no stranger to the concept of seeking relief with the nearest willing warm body, but the key word there was *willing*. Not someone whose unconscious body happened to be within reaching distance of his erection.

"You shouldn't," Alex started, but couldn't find the rest of the words. Sometimes it was as if he had a hard time knowing what he was feeling, and the more he was feeling, the harder it was to put it into words.

Daniel sat up and looked at him, eyes searching. "I shouldn't what?"

"You shouldn't let people take advantage of you." That wasn't exactly what was wrong, but it was true, at least, and it was something Alex worried about every day. Daniel was too kind, too generous, too easygoing for his own good.

"Like you'd ever take advantage of me."

"Apparently, you're ready to let anyone do whatever they want to you!"

Daniel let out a startled laugh. "Is that what you think is happening here?"

That was one of those questions you weren't meant to answer, because yes, obviously Alex thought that was what was happening or he wouldn't have said so. He grabbed a change of clothing and stormed off to the shower, not emerging until he thought he could stay composed. When he got out, Daniel was dressed, his shoes already on. This was an unprecedented hour for Daniel to be awake, and Alex was ready to tell him to go back to sleep and let himself out when he woke up.

But Daniel spoke first. "Want to go out to breakfast? You still have an hour before you need to be at work."

Every instinct told Alex to say no, to go directly to work because then he wouldn't have to think about what happened. He wouldn't even have to think about why he didn't want to think about it. He could just pretend it hadn't happened, and when he saw Daniel later, Daniel would do the same thing, smoothing over any of Alex's awkwardness.

But that was what he had done after Paul's comment the

other night, and it hadn't worked. It had done nothing to help him stop thinking of what Paul had said, had done worse than nothing to help him stop thinking about how much he wished Paul had been right. Instead, he had nearly made things awkward with Daniel.

"Okay," Alex said. "Let's have breakfast." He looked away when Daniel's face lit up.

* * *

Daniel waited until they had both finished their breakfast and were waiting for the check. That way Alex could make a quick getaway if he needed to.

"I want to talk about what happened earlier," Daniel said, in exactly the same tone he'd used when, a few minutes earlier, he had said, "I want a bite of your pancakes."

Alex looked away. "I'm sorry. I can't apologize enough."

The diner was noisy. Still, Daniel lowered his voice. "I mean the part where I offered to have sex with you and you seemed to think I was either debasing myself or volunteering to be assaulted."

"That is not what happened."

Daniel raised his eyebrows. "You sure about that?" He gave Alex time to think through what had happened, knowing that Alex would probably remember every syllable they had spoken.

"I thought you were offering to let me use you to, um, rub off on you," Alex said to his coffee cup.

"Yep," Daniel agreed, deciding not to comment on Alex's use of the word "use" because there was sexy using and very unsexy using and that was a whole different conversation. "Doesn't mean I wouldn't have enjoyed it. I want to make it really clear that I was into it. You weren't hurting me or violating me or anything."

Alex was quiet again. Daniel wasn't sure whether he realized exactly how much Daniel was admitting to when he said that he would have enjoyed it.

"Thank you for telling me," Alex finally said, addressing the words more to the maple syrup remaining on his plate than to Daniel.

"That doesn't mean *you* were into it, though, and I'm sorry your body tricked you while you were asleep, if that's what happened."

"That's not what happened. I was awake."

Daniel had figured as much, but wanted to go through this incident step by step before Alex really started to worry. The fact was that similar things had happened to Daniel before—share a bed with someone and there's a chance you'll have unwanted or unintended contact—but telling Alex that something was perfectly normal and nothing to worry about had never, not once, succeeded in making him believe that something was normal and nothing to worry about. "Normal" was not a concept that mattered to Aleksander Savchenko in any meaningful way, and that was one of the things Daniel loved best about him as a friend and as—well, as a friend. That was all that mattered at the moment.

However, if Alex had been awake, there was a chance that Alex had wanted that contact with Daniel. He had been trying not to think too much about that possibility, not to read intention into what might have been an instinctive physical response.

The prudent thing would be to change the topic, Daniel knew. Just because Alex, maybe, on some level, wasn't opposed to the idea of sex with Daniel, that didn't mean that he wanted to do anything about it. But if he did want to do something about it, he would never act on it without prompting. Alex, given a choice, played it safe every time. Daniel, though, wasn't particularly interested in safety; maybe it was because he had been coddled and spoiled all his life, or maybe it was because the last five or so years had been an object lesson for his entire generation about just how short and brutal life can be. In any case, he didn't even have to think very hard about it. He knew that he needed to try; he needed to at least open the door if there was a chance Alex wanted to walk through it.

"I meant what I said earlier," Daniel said, aiming for casual. He was pretty sure he achieved "not desperate," at least. "We could do that sort of thing, if you wanted. It doesn't have to be a big deal. It can just be—I mean, it's nicer with a friend."

Alex glanced up, startled, but immediately returned his gaze to the table. "I wouldn't know. I don't make it a practice to sleep with all my friends."

Daniel supposed that the implication was that Daniel did make it a practice to sleep with his friends, which wasn't true—case in point, present company—but wasn't far off the mark, either. "Are you—are you calling me promiscuous?" he asked, a little incredulously. "Do you have a problem with—"

"No. Obviously not." Alex rubbed the bridge of his nose, plainly looking for the right words. "My experience isn't the same as yours. That's all. For one, you and Mary are my only friends, and you have dozens of friends in the city alone. Throw a dart and you'll find a friend happy to go to bed with you."

"Don't let Paul hear you say that he doesn't qualify as your friend. He'd cry."

Alex made a scoffing sound and finally looked up from his plate. "Paul tolerates me for Mary's sake."

"In that case, he's been tolerating you for eight years. He tolerated you being a groomsman at his wedding. He'll probably tolerate his kids calling you Uncle Alex. That's a lot of toleration."

Alex's cheeks were pink. "Let's go back to talking about your terrible promiscuity."

Daniel snorted. "Fine. If you want to be promiscuous with me, you're welcome to. That's all." He wasn't expecting an answer; he wasn't even expecting Alex to do anything other than change the topic.

"Okay," Alex said.

Daniel's eyebrows shot up. "Okay?"

"No. I mean—I understand what you're saying. I don't know what to do with it yet."

"Fair," Daniel said, and nudged Alex's foot under the table.

Chapter Six

"I'm going up to Cape Cod to see my grandmother next weekend," Daniel said when they were out to dinner on Friday night. "Want to come? I'd like it if you came, but I won't be upset if you say no."

Alex knew Daniel visited his grandmother a few times a year. He also knew Daniel couldn't stand his grandmother, maybe legitimately hated her, and the fact that he went anyway, to check on an elderly woman who had alienated her entire family, made Alex simultaneously want to shake him and—well—maybe give him a hug. He wasn't sure about that last thing.

Nobody else was willing to check on Daniel's grandmother. His father hadn't spoken to Mrs. Cabot in over ten years. Daniel's aunts and uncles were all in one way or another estranged from their mother; his cousins were scattered around the globe.

On Christmas, various members of Daniel's family had descended on New York and Alex had been more or less abducted to have dinner with them. They had all been planning some outing for the following day when Daniel said he'd need to beg off in order to visit his grandmother.

"Somebody has to," Daniel had explained when everyone

around the table exchanged worried glances.

"You stay and have fun, darling. I'll go check on her myself," Daniel's mother had said.

"No," everyone other than Alex had said at once.

"You'll kill her," Daniel's father pointed out. "She'll say one ugly thing and you'll be right there with a pillow over her face."

"You say that like it's a bad thing," said Daniel's mother.

"None of us have the cash to bail you out," said the other woman.

Daniel's mother appeared to consider this. "I have the cash, though."

"She disowned my father when he came out to her," Daniel had explained when they were alone. Alex had appreciated the privacy, because he wouldn't have known how to arrange his face when hearing that news. Disowning wasn't a surprise, nor was Daniel's father being gay—Alex might have picked up on that even if Daniel hadn't told him so outright months earlier when he found Alex looking at a framed photograph of Mr. Cabot with another man, their arms around one another's shoulders, the sea in the distance.

It was the idea of it all being out in the open that surprised Alex. He was almost positive his mother knew he was queer, because if she didn't, she'd be on his case about getting married. But they didn't talk about it. Well, they didn't talk about much. They talked about articles they had read in *Scientific American* and the best way to treat ulcers. He had no complaints and doubted she did, either.

Maybe there was something to be said for laying out all your secrets and making people choose between accepting you and getting out of your life. The idea made Alex feel acutely ill.

But Daniel's parents were—well, it came as no surprise to

Alex that they had raised a son who did whatever he pleased.

And apparently what pleased him was to check on this grandmother they all despised. Perhaps *pleased* was too strong a word; perhaps *despised* was as well. But either way, Daniel drove up to Cape Cod every few months. When he came back, he had a kind of forced cheerfulness about him that was somehow worse than when he was just plain sad.

"You want me to go with you?" Alex asked, confused. He didn't know why Daniel would want him to come along. It couldn't be for the pleasure of Alex's company, because Alex was peevish and difficult whenever he left Manhattan. His sister had moved out to Brighton Beach when she got married, their parents following as soon as their first grandchild was born, and that was about as far as Alex would willingly travel. Well, semi-willingly, since he tended to grumble the entire time. And Daniel knew this perfectly well, because he had been coming with Alex on all those visits since about two months after they met, for reasons that were unclear to Alex.

"I'm inviting you," Daniel said. "You can say no."

That wasn't what Daniel had said, though. He had said that he'd like it if Alex came along. Alex knew he could say no and that Daniel wouldn't hold it against him. And that's what Alex knew he should do. He should stay home. One, because he hated traveling. Two, because he still hadn't figured out what to do about Daniel's suggestion that they could just...have sex. He had suggested it with the same neutral kindness he employed to suggest trying the new Bangladeshi restaurant or watching *Masterpiece Theater*. Maybe that was how sex worked with Daniel. It probably was. Hell, it sometimes was even for Alex.

But when Alex thought about sex with Daniel—which was

now, unfortunately, something he was doing with increasing frequency—he didn't feel casual about it. He wanted to stop thinking about it, wanted to stop thinking about how it had felt—however briefly, however spuriously—to have Daniel in his arms. That moment, and the conversation that followed it at breakfast, had called up all the thoughts that Alex had so diligently ignored for the past year, all the silly imaginings of what Daniel could be to him in another world, if Alex were a different person. Now, when he saw Daniel, he knew what it felt like to hold him, and he knew that the potential for sex, at least, existed between them; it was impossible to train his thoughts in safer directions.

He shouldn't spend the weekend with Daniel, that much was clear. But it was getting more and more difficult to deny Daniel anything he wanted, because making Daniel happy so often made Alex happy.

"Okay," Alex said. "I have that weekend off." Technically, he had every weekend off, but that week he'd have off Friday too, because Mary pointed out that it was all well and good for the pair of them to work as much as they wanted, but the office staff needed holidays.

Daniel's face lit up. Really, he was far too pleased about having Alex's company for a weekend.

"If we leave at nine, we'll get there in the middle of the afternoon," Daniel said.

The sensible thing would be to leave at seven and totally avoid morning rush hour, but nine o'clock for Daniel was close to five a.m. for people who kept civilized schedules. And it wouldn't do to have Daniel asleep behind the wheel.

"Okay," Alex said. "Nine o'clock," he added, as if Daniel would be picking him up tomorrow, rather than in a week. The words hung there, neither of them saying anything, Daniel smiling goofily, Alex startled to realize he might be smiling too.

* * *

One of the reasons Daniel chose this neighborhood was that he had doubted either of his parents would drop in. And he was right about one of his parents: his mother said it was in poor taste to promenade (her word) in expensive clothing through sad (also her word) neighborhoods, and therefore she developed the habit of calling Daniel from the phone at an Italian restaurant near Tompkins Square Park and waiting for him to arrive, as if she were simply buzzing up from the lobby of his building.

His father, though, just drove right up to Daniel's building, parallel parked his embarrassing old boat of a car, and started chatting with Daniel's neighbors. It was horrible. Once, Daniel had come downstairs to find him flirting with old Mrs. Rosenstein and burping somebody's baby. Daniel still didn't know where the baby had come from. It wasn't even like Hartford was nearby. It was a two-hour drive when there wasn't any traffic, and the one thing you could count on was that there would be plenty of traffic.

Daniel had been up half the night putting the finishing touches on an article. When the sun came up he was still mostly awake, so he went outside and hauled some bricks and rubble to make a border for the garden bed where Blanca had planted sunflower seeds. It was mindless work, just balancing rocks on top of larger rocks and hoping for the best, but the weather was mild and he could hear David Bowie's new album through somebody's open window, so all in all it was a good morning.

"Looks like you're making progress there," came a voice he should have expected.

"Hi, Dad." Daniel stood and wiped his hands on his jeans. "You could call before coming, you know."

"I did. Three hours ago, and then again twenty minutes ago." His father was leaning against the length of chain link fence that still partially blocked the garden from the sidewalk. "You didn't pick up. Then I called Alex at the clinic, but he said he hadn't seen you. So I figured that you'd be here."

"He isn't my secretary, you know."

"No, that he isn't," said his father. "I had the morning free, so I thought I'd bring the car."

"Oh. Thanks." Daniel usually took the train up to Hartford, stopped by Dad and Everett's house to get the car, and then drove out to Cape Cod. The next day he repeated the process in reverse. But apparently this time he was driving directly from New York. "Why?"

"Aren't I allowed to want to see my own son?"

"I saw you two weeks ago. Don't you have a job?"

His father grimaced and wavered his hand in a so-so gesture that made Daniel laugh despite himself. His father did something in Connecticut regarding funding for public housing, a job that had kept him pretty busy until a Republican was elected governor.

"Let me take a shower and I can get you a drink?" Daniel offered.

"No need," his father said. "Alex said I could park the car in that loading bay behind the clinic and it would be safe until you need it on Friday. I'll do that, then take you out to lunch, unless you have a better offer?"

CHAPTER SIX

When he walked into the restaurant an hour later, Daniel probably shouldn't have been surprised to find Alex already sitting at the table with his father. Daniel's father was annoyingly persuasive (unless you were a Republican governor, apparently). He wondered if his father timed his visit to coincide exactly with the half hour Alex took for lunch at precisely 12:30. He wouldn't put it past him.

"You've never met my mother, have you?" Dad asked Alex, even though he had to know the answer. "She's—just don't take anything she says seriously, all right? Or, rather, take it seriously, but understand that she's a vicious old bat and quite possibly the devil's mouthpiece and nobody with any taste or judgment agrees with two consecutive words she says."

"He's already heard Mom threaten to murder her," Daniel pointed out. "He knows what he's getting himself into."

"Yes, but that's your mother. Alex probably knows better than to take her murder threats seriously."

"I always take them seriously, sir," Alex said, and Daniel hoped his father appreciated how rare it was for Alex to joke with anyone other than him or Mary. At least, he was pretty sure it was a joke.

"I know that Daniel's grandmother is a bigot," Alex went on. "I'm going for moral support, not to pay any attention to her."

Daniel was sort of taken aback. "I don't need moral support. I've been visiting her on my own for years. I'm used to everything she says."

They both frowned at him. Oh, for God's sake. She was an old lady who had managed to fuck up her life so spectacularly that nobody particularly cared whether she lived or died—except, presumably, those of her children who were listed in her will. Daniel pitied her, because he would never be in that situation.

There were plenty of people who loved him, and the fact that his grandmother wasn't among them didn't really matter.

When Alex left to go back to work, Daniel's father sighed and waved over the waiter to order a bottle of wine. "What do I have to do to get Alex to call me Tom or Thomas or Tommy or 'hey you' or really anything other than sir? He calls Everett by his first name."

"That's because Everett threatened to call him Dr. Savchenko if he didn't."

"Sneaky. Nice."

"He calls Mom Patricia, but that's because they're best pals." Daniel wrinkled his nose. "It's terrible. They talk on the phone. They go *shopping.* No, Dad, that wasn't a suggestion." Daniel had initially greeted the friendship between his mother and Alex with a kind of stupefied horror: the last thing he wanted was this man he had embarrassing feelings for to get close with the one person on earth who would embarrass him without effort or compunction. He didn't understand what they could possibly have in common, and it only horrified him more when he saw that the thing they had in common was *him.*

"When do I get to meet his parents?" Daniel's father asked.

Daniel knew this trick. His father wasn't asking *whether*, he was asking *when*, the same strategy he deployed to get politicians to agree to unlikely things. "Why do you want to?"

"It seems to me that he's family."

That was brutal, because it wasn't like Daniel could deny that he thought of Alex as family, and he couldn't deny that his family thought of Alex as family, and he also couldn't deny that he thought of Alex's family as his family. "You know we're not together, right?"

"You're always together," his father said, which, dammit,

was almost exactly what Daniel had thought to himself during that dinner with Paul and Mary.

"Don't redefine terms in the middle of a conversation."

"Dan, it doesn't really matter what you call it. He's important to you. That's all I care about."

And it wasn't as if Daniel could really argue with that.

* * *

Alex hadn't known what he expected Daniel to wear to visit his grandmother, but it wasn't jeans with a hole in the knee, a pair of heavy black boots, and a black T-shirt with an inexplicable mushroom on the front along with the name of a band. His hair was tied back into a haphazard little ponytail, which somehow looked even more subversive than when it was loose around his face. When it was loose, you could explain it away as laziness or a rare phobia relating to barbershops, but like this, it was a choice.

Alex had on charcoal-gray cotton trousers, a white oxford, and the dove-gray sweater that Daniel's mother got him for Christmas. He shaved extra carefully that morning, because even possibly evil grandmothers were still grandmothers.

"You're such a kiss-up," Daniel said when Alex told him as much. "I'm taking you to meet the worst person and you got yourself all prettied up."

"You have so many nicer outfits," Alex lamented. "And instead you're wearing what you garden in. People are going to think I'm your parole officer."

Daniel laughed, which probably wasn't safe to do in traffic. This had to be why Alex paid such close attention to him, the way his fingers curved around the wheel, the dimple that appeared during his biggest smiles, the strands of honey and gold that appeared in his hair in the summer.

After two hours they stopped for breakfast (well, breakfast for Daniel; for Alex and everybody else it was lunch).

Alex had never learned how to drive. He had spent his entire adult life in New York City and could count on two hands the number of times he had ever even ridden in a car that wasn't a taxicab. He would have thought, though, that time in city cabs might have gotten him used to the worst kind of driving. Nothing could have prepared him for what happened almost as soon as they crossed the border into Massachusetts.

"You have turn signals. You're supposed to use them," Alex said, his hand braced against the roof of the car. "Why are you honking? Why are you so close to that car?"

Daniel changed lanes in a move that had Alex double-checking his lap belt and swearing.

"Was that Ukrainian? Are you swearing at me in Ukrainian?"

"I'm praying," Alex lied primly.

Daniel didn't seem to be committing any infractions that other drivers weren't also committing, and it was possible that anyone driving like a sane and responsible person would be instantly run off the road, but none of this made Alex feel any safer.

"Who taught you how to drive?" Alex asked after they escaped an especially harrowing roundabout. "It was your mother, wasn't it? I bet it was your mother."

"I'm telling her you said that," Daniel laughed.

"She'll take it as a compliment."

"She takes everything you say as a compliment," Daniel complained, before abruptly hitting the brakes and flinging an arm across Alex's chest, as if one arm, however sturdy, was going to do anything to prevent him from cracking his head on the dashboard. Daniel kept his arm there, though, even after they weren't in imminent danger of fiery death, and Alex found one of his own hands drifting up to touch it where it rested against his thudding heart. He let his fingers brush against the back of Daniel's wrist, almost brief enough to be deniable, or it would have been if he hadn't made the mistake of turning his head to look at Daniel while he was doing it.

"You should probably keep your eyes on the road," Alex said when he found Daniel looking back at him.

Daniel flashed him a confusing smile and, thank God, returned his attention to the road and both hands to the wheel.

"This is nothing. Remind me never to bring you to Boston," Daniel said. "At least not in a car. You'd die of the shock."

"I'd die of the impact," Alex grumbled.

The scenery began to change at around the same time the drivers appeared to return to their senses. He could see water outside his window—not a pretty sea view, but it was water anyway. The other day, uncomfortable with the prospect of visiting a place he couldn't even locate on the globe, Alex had borrowed Mary's road atlas and looked at a map of Massachusetts. He knew that this was water was a bay or a sound; he had looked up *bay* and *sound* in the dictionary, then *strait* and *inlet*, and still he hadn't been able to picture the place he was going to visit.

He hadn't seen much of America and hardly remembered anything that came before it—a village, a town, a city, another city, all marked by different schools and different languages more than any sense of where he was in the world. The sensible grid of Manhattan had come as a relief, and whenever he left it, he felt a vague uneasiness, as if he might find himself in another strange place, have to learn another language.

But Daniel's presence kept him grounded, the restless thrumming of his fingers on the steering wheel a reminder of the present. They weren't on a highway anymore, or even an especially busy road, and Daniel started pointing out landmarks—if "a really good hot dog stand" or "the drive-in where I lost my virginity" counted as landmarks. There were also the things he didn't point out, probably because they were fixtures of the landscape that Daniel had long since stopped noticing: lighthouses, sand dunes covered in long sea grass, houses built of faded gray wood.

And then Daniel was pulling into a curved driveway that led to a house hidden from the road. It was a large house—all houses were large by Alex's Manhattan standards—but it wasn't what movies and television had taught him to consider a mansion. It had a sort of haphazard effect, as if it hadn't been built all at once, the grayish white of the painted wood the only thing unifying what might otherwise seem like different structures slapped hastily together.

Daniel drove around the back of the house and parked.

"I called yesterday to let Magda know I was coming and bringing a guest, but I don't know if she told Grandmother."

"Magda?"

"The housekeeper. There's also a nurse. There's a gardener too, but he's about eighty and I don't think he does much of anything anymore."

Alex opened the car door and was hit with the smell of sea air, different somehow than what he was used to from Coney Island and Brighton Beach. He could hear the ocean, too—it had to be right over those dunes.

Daniel unlocked the trunk and handed Alex his suitcase—Alex hadn't known what to pack, and so even though they were only staying one night, he had managed to fill a suitcase—then took out his own canvas bag, which couldn't be large enough to fit more than a spare shirt and pair of pajamas.

"Ready?" Daniel asked.

"If you are," Alex said.

Daniel bumped his shoulder against Alex's then led the way into the house.

Chapter Seven

Because they came in the back door, the first person they saw was Magda, who was smoking while stirring a pot on the stove. When she saw Daniel, she dropped both the spoon and the cigarette in the sink and went to wrap him up in a hug. She smelled like tobacco smoke and baby powder, a peculiar combination that Daniel would always associate with summers at this house.

"She's awake," Magda said. "But if you creep up the stairs like little mice she won't hear you. That will buy you some time."

Daniel introduced Alex, who immediately spoke to Magda in what Daniel assumed was Polish, as that was Magda's native language. Magda responded with something that made Alex smile ruefully as he held up his thumb and forefinger in the universal symbol for "not much."

"Since when do you speak Polish?" Daniel asked as they went upstairs. He knew Alex spoke Ukrainian, obviously, and what he described as "a little Russian" but which was enough for him to carry on a conversation, as well as some Spanish.

"I really don't. Just a few words."

"It looks like Magda got this room ready for you," Daniel

said, opening a door into one of the spare rooms. "I'm next door. I'm going to go deal with my grandmother while you unpack or lie down or whatever."

Alex frowned. "Wait for me."

"You really don't need to. Magda won't tell her I brought anyone. Save yourself," he said, trying to make a joke of it."

"Wait for me," Alex repeated.

So Daniel went back down to the kitchen and sat with Magda. "Handsome," Magda said. "And a nice boy."

"He's a doctor," Daniel said, aware that he was absolutely showing Alex off for his grandmother's housekeeper. But Magda had been a fixture in his life for as long as he remembered, much more so than his grandmother or any of his aunts or uncles, often feeding and looking after as many as a dozen Cabot cousins every summer.

"A doctor," Magda said approvingly. "It's good that you brought someone. It's bad that you come at all, but it's good that you don't come alone."

"If I didn't come, how would I see you?" He asked Magda about her own grandchildren until the nurse—a new one, of course, as the old one had sensibly decided to quit—came in saying that Mrs. Cabot wanted something, so Daniel was left alone in the kitchen until Alex came down.

Daniel had really hoped his grandmother would be drowsy, or maybe just spontaneously motivated to be civil, but no, she was awake and alert and filled with bright ideas about how to be horrible.

In the space of half an hour, she told Daniel that it was a pity he took after his mother and hadn't inherited the Cabot good looks, instead—she feared—only sharing his father's degeneracy. It was a pity Daniel wasn't taller, wasn't married, had to have braces for so long, never played football, hadn't gone to law school, and dressed like a vagrant. She asked if Alex was an Eastern European agitator, then asked why he hadn't gone into a more prestigious specialty than pediatrics, and then asked what his parents did. She wanted to know if Daniel had gotten a real job and proceeded to cry when he cheerfully told her that he hadn't. Still sobbing, she began to enumerate the failings of each of her children, then her grandchildren, then reminded Daniel that he wasn't in the will.

That was when the nurse announced that it was time for Mrs. Cabot to turn in for the night.

"That wasn't as bad as I expected," Daniel said, relieved, once he and Alex were alone in the sitting room.

"No," Alex said.

"No, what?"

"It was bad. If you were expecting worse, that says bad things about you." His accent had crept into his voice at some point. Usually there was only the faintest trace of it unless he was exhausted or had spent the day with his family.

"I warned you what she was like."

"You don't look like your father? Is she blind? Well, she's very old so maybe she is, but in that case she's foolish to pretend she can see. And she calls your father names in front of strangers? Was she always like this? Do your parents know she's this bad?"

Daniel remembered her being decent to him when he was a kid, but he couldn't say more than that. Even though he had spent his summers here, he had spent most of his time with his cousins, not his grandmother.

"She was always like this, but not to me. According to my father, she always fought with my aunts, and then when they stopped talking to her, she turned on other people."

"All these other relatives, they all had the sense to go away? And now there's only you left? Why do you have to be the punching bag?"

Daniel got to his feet. He had heard all of this from both his parents and had been hearing it for years. "Let's get a drink."

"I don't want a drink. I want to take you away from here." Alex had color in his usually pale cheeks. He was angry—not cranky, not peeved, but actually upset. Daniel felt bad about that—he never wanted Alex to be upset, and he should have insisted that Alex stay away from his grandmother. But the damage was done, and he wasn't willing to have yet another person try to explain that his grandmother was a horrible person, a fact he had known for most of his life.

"Well, a drink is what I'm offering," he said gently, because ultimately the only reason Alex was upset was because he cared about Daniel. "I know you think I'm being masochistic or whatever, and you can call my mom and vent at her about it. She'll love it. Coca-Cola, or something stronger? There's loads of wine. Probably it's expensive and it would be a shame if a pair of degenerate communist agitators enjoyed it."

Alex gave him a look Daniel didn't understand—some combination of fond and tired, maybe—but finally sighed. "Fancy wine, please."

Daniel chose a bottle of wine at random, then grabbed wine glasses from the china cabinet and led the way outside. On the porch, they sat on a pair of Adirondack chairs. Alex was mostly quiet, but not the irritated kind of quiet, so Daniel kept up a one-sided conversation while they drank. "I don't want to ask Magda to cook for us, and I doubt there's anything we'd want to eat here anyway, so would you mind walking into town for dinner? There's an ice cream shop, too."

"You don't have to entertain me. I'm not here on vacation."

"You sort of are, though. I mean, it's a place people do come on vacation, and just because I brought you here to be abused to your face doesn't mean you need to have a horrible time. I'm really sorry she said those things to you, by the way. I don't think I apologized before."

Alex made a frustrated sound and waved his hand dismissively. "She's a stranger to me. I've heard worse from better people than her. I don't care about her opinions. But you were bothered. I know I'm not good at reading people's moods, but I do know you, Daniel."

Daniel opened his mouth to deny it, but he had decided a while ago not to lie to Alex, and he wasn't going to start now. "You're right. I mean, she really fucked my father up, so part of me is glad that she reaped what she sowed, but the whole situation could have been avoided if she just chose to be decent. She didn't have any reason not to be. There's already plenty of shittiness in the world and she adds to it *optionally.* Now can we talk about literally anything else?"

Alex stared at him for long enough that Daniel wondered what he had said.

When the wine was gone, they took a slightly tipsy walk into town to get pizza and ice cream. It was a pretty town, its sidewalks reliably crowded with tourists and locals at the height of the summer, but still relatively empty now. Alex might think this wasn't a vacation, but as far as Daniel knew, Alex had never taken a vacation. He claimed that he never wanted to, preferring his routine, which Daniel understood. And the fact that Daniel understood it made him appreciate even more that Alex had decided to come with him this time, and made him even more determined that Alex not have a horrible time.

There was enough of a breeze that Alex's usually smooth hair was ruffled, and Daniel knew his own had to be a bird's nest. He tried to shove it behind his ears, but the pieces that were too short to reach his rubber band kept flying loose. Alex was sneaking looks, but not, Daniel thought, because he was disappointed in Daniel's messy hair.

They hadn't talked about sleeping together since that conversation a week ago, and Daniel had pretty much taken that to mean Alex wasn't interested—which was disappointing but not really a change from the status quo, so Daniel was trying not to think about it. But when he caught Alex looking at him, it was a new sort of look, as if he were seeing Daniel in a new way, or maybe just letting himself see.

By the time they came back to the house, the sun had nearly set. Alex went upstairs while Daniel set about making sure Magda and the nurse were being paid correctly and that they had his and his father's phone numbers if they ever needed references. The lawyer was supposed to deal with all that, but it never hurt to double-check.

When Daniel went upstairs, he found the door to Alex's room ajar but no sounds or movement coming from within. He gently pushed the door open a bit more and saw Alex on the bed, dressed except for his shoes, his eyes shut. Daniel paused on the threshold and took in the rare sight of Alex asleep, his hair mussed, his face relaxed. He always carried so much tension, even when he seemed fine, but seeing him like this drove home how tightly wound he usually was.

Daniel stepped into the room and sat carefully on the edge of the bed. "Alex." He put his hand on Alex's shoulder but didn't shake him, not sure if that would startle him. "Come on.

You'll be furious if you fall asleep without brushing your teeth. And it's only eight o'clock. You'll be awake at a godawful hour tomorrow."

Alex's eyes opened, and Daniel watched, his heart for some reason in his throat, as Alex realized where he was and who he was with. He looked—he looked happy, and Daniel found himself smiling down at him.

"Did you really pass out after two glasses of wine?"

"I passed out from the trauma of driving with you," Alex said, his voice a little thick.

"You're going to be so mad at yourself if you fall asleep now. Let's get up and go for a walk."

"We just took a walk," Alex mumbled, sounding half asleep. He dropped a hand over Daniel's where it still rested on his shoulder. Daniel couldn't tell whether he even realized he was doing it, but remembered he had done something similar in the car. Alex initiating a touch was something new, and even if it didn't mean anything, it was rare enough that Daniel wouldn't take it for granted.

"Since when did you get lazy?" Daniel asked. "Come on, you haven't seen the beach. You've got to at least put your feet in the water."

"Fine," Alex grumbled, but he squeezed Daniel's hand before he got up.

* * *

Alex had never been to a beach that wasn't loud and crowded to the point of being his personal vision of hell, like if the stickiest summertime rush hour on the subway somehow came with both the promise of sunburn and a higher than usual chance of being flashed. Worse than that, even, because you still had to take a steamy and crowded subway home from Coney Island while you were caked in sand. Disgusting. His skin crawled just thinking about it.

But the beach here was empty, and Alex didn't know if that was because it was owned by the Cabots or because it was dark and a little too chilly for most people to think about going to the beach. Daniel had put on his leather jacket and Alex wore his sweater. Alex thought he might have warmer feelings about the beach if it were always this empty, quiet, and cool.

"Oh, I know," Daniel said when Alex told him as much. "There's a reason Mary and I never bother asking if you want to come to the beach with us. Turns out that all you need is a private beach on the estate of an evil witch to make you happy." He laid a plaid woolen blanket out on the sand and sat on it, patting the spot beside him.

Alex frowned as he sat next to Daniel. "I know that I'm difficult to please."

"What? I wasn't teasing you. You really aren't hard to please at all." He wrapped his arms around his knees and turned to face Alex. "There are so many things that you like so much. You like vanilla ice cream and pepperoni pizza. You like Eric Clapton—"

"I really don't—"

"You love Eric Clapton," Daniel said, starting to laugh, a warm, easy laugh that Alex knew was at his expense but also, somehow, not. "You love him so much. And you like his music too. But I'll keep your secret safe."

"Such a liar." Alex didn't trust himself to look at Daniel's smiling face, so he looked out at the sea, the moonlight glinting off the water.

"You like quiet. You like time to yourself. You like complaining about sports."

"That's not liking. That's disliking."

"No, you love it. If I started complaining about baseball right now your eyes would light up. You like kids even when they're awful. You like your family in two-hour increments. And it turns out that you even found something to like on a trip that you probably didn't expect to enjoy at all."

It wasn't as if Alex didn't know all those things, but he tended to frame it as the reverse: he disliked all ice cream other than plain vanilla and any pizza that involved vegetables, he could hardly tolerate noise and didn't like spending time with most people. He had a hard time being around his family for prolonged periods, even though he loved them and missed seeing them between visits. Added up like that, it made him sound fussy and impossible.

But everything Daniel said was true. Alex did like all those things. He was just so used to his preferences—his needs, even—being out of sync with what everyone else seemed to want, that he started to think of himself as joyless and sour. As a disappointment.

Logically, he already knew that Daniel didn't think of him that way, that Daniel had to enjoy spending time with him, considering the fact that he did it so often. And he knew that Mary had to like him too, because otherwise she wouldn't have wanted to start a practice with him after accumulating years of evidence of what he was like. As for his parents, he knew they would love him even if he were a nightmare to be around, so he didn't take their love as any kind of evidence as to his character.

But hearing it laid out the way Daniel had done made him

feel like his quirks weren't even remarkable.

Alex thought about what the day had looked like: Eric Clapton on the eight-track player in Daniel's car, vanilla ice cream and pepperoni pizza for dinner. Time to himself in a quiet room. A trip to the beach under optimal conditions. He hadn't even realized he was being given those things.

"You like when people say what they mean," Daniel went on. "You like sitting in the back row at the movies. You like having your own popcorn so other people can load theirs up with butter and salt without contaminating yours. You like movies about aliens. You like—"

"I like you," Alex said. He turned in time to see Daniel go still. It was dark, and Daniel was tan from working outside, but Alex would bet he was blushing. "I like you so much."

Daniel didn't say anything, but there was a tiny, pleased smile working at the edges of his mouth. He leaned over, slow, as if he were giving Alex time to understand what was happening, time to move away, and kissed him high on his cheek, right on his cheekbone, so that when Alex's eyes closed, his eyelashes touched Daniel's nose. Then he kissed the corner of Alex's mouth before pulling away.

"I like you too," Daniel said, only loud enough to be heard over the waves lapping against the shore, and it probably said something that Alex believed him, hadn't doubted it in a long time.

"Look at the stars," Daniel said, lying down on the blanket. "We're too close to Boston to see much of anything, but it's clearer than it'll ever be in New York."

And so Alex lay down, careful to keep his head on the blanket, because sand on his pillow would make it impossible to sleep, and looked up at the sky. They looked at stars that neither of them could identify, and then when they went back to the house, Daniel squeezed his shoulder at the door to Alex's room. "Go to sleep. You must be exhausted."

Alex was, and so he did.

* * *

The next morning, Daniel stumbled downstairs, still bleary-eyed and half asleep, to find Alex already awake and dressed, which was not a surprise, and drinking coffee at the kitchen table with Magda, which sort of was a surprise. Alex didn't usually bother with small talk—he wasn't rude, but it cost him an effort that it didn't cost most people. When Daniel got closer, he could hear that Magda was talking about her oldest grandchild, who was in medical school.

An hour later, Daniel kissed his grandmother on the cheek, pretending not to hear a word she said. Then he hugged Magda goodbye, split another pot of strong coffee with Alex, and got in the car.

"Want to hit that hot dog stand?" Daniel asked.

"It's not even eleven o'clock in the morning."

"That's not a no."

They bought a pair of hot dogs and ate them over by the lighthouse, at what was probably supposed to be a scenic viewpoint but which was mainly where seagulls harassed tourists for food. But even the seagulls seemed to be taking it easy this weekend, and they were left to eat their breakfast in peaceful silence.

Kissing him last night had almost been comfortable, the soft skin of Alex's cheek new under his lips but somehow not unfamiliar. When his mouth brushed a faint roughness, he knew it was the barely perceptible white-blond stubble that he could only glimpse in bright sunlight. When Alex exhaled, it was the same sound as when he settled Daniel against his side on the sofa.

It would have been easy to slide his lips across Alex's, to make the kiss something else, maybe even to try again when they were upstairs, but he didn't want to push. He wanted to give Alex every opportunity to get used to the idea of it.

He sort of expected Alex to act weird about it, but the kiss had only been just on the far side of friendly, so maybe Alex was pretending it had never happened. Except that didn't sound like Alex at all. He must have liked it, because he wasn't great at concealing his reactions to things he didn't like. Daniel knew he had to ask, but this was close enough to topics that made Alex jumpy and Daniel wanted to tread carefully.

"Was it okay when I kissed you?" Daniel asked in between bites of hot dog, careful not to attempt eye contact. "Thumbs up, thumbs down, or jury still out?"

"Thumbs up," Alex said, after only a tiny hesitation.

"Good." Daniel managed not to grin. Managed not to kiss Alex again right there, either. "I need more coffee. An entire bucket would be nice, but I'd settle for a cup."

"Coffee and hot dogs do not go together."

"Not with that attitude they don't."

Back in the car, a reasonable non-bucket-sized quantity of coffee later, they almost immediately hit traffic.

"Probably an accident," Daniel said. "There's no reason for traffic heading out of Cape Cod on a Saturday morning." And sure enough, forty-five minutes later they passed a fender bender. The road was clear for all of ten minutes, and then the traffic again slowed to a crawl.

It was like that for the next two hours, and by the time one o'clock rolled around, they were barely in New Bedford. Alex flicked through the radio stations, trying to find a traffic report, but he wasn't having any luck.

Daniel found himself shifting in his seat, increasingly frustrated with being trapped in a car that was stuck in bumper-to-bumper traffic. Objectively, it was not a problem. Neither of them had anywhere to be all day and they weren't in any danger of running out of gas. Still, he was ready to chew his arm off.

"You're squirming," Alex pointed out.

"Sorry," Daniel mumbled and tried to sit still.

"No, I mean, let's stop for lunch. Maybe someone will know what's going on or can tell us about a detour."

Daniel wasn't hungry, but he wanted to put some distance between himself and that fucking highway, so as soon as the traffic inched along far enough that he could see an exit, he turned off in the direction of the waterfront. There would have to be restaurants there.

"This is pretty," Alex said when Daniel parked.

"It is, isn't it? If you're interested in whaling, abolitionism, textile mills, or Quakers, this is the place for you." Summers on Cape Cod had involved day trips to local museums, and Daniel had the disjointed trivia to prove it.

"Whaling," Alex repeated, sounding revolted.

"Sorry about the traffic."

"I don't care about the traffic. I'm not the one driving in it. You, though." He looked closely at Daniel. "It's good that we stopped."

Daniel felt less murderous after eating a lobster roll, but the waitress's news about the traffic was all bad. "The road into

Providence is backed up for miles," she said. "Construction."

"I took that road eastbound yesterday," Daniel said, as if this would change anything. The waitress only shrugged.

"There was construction equipment parked on the side of the road yesterday," Alex said. Across the table, he was peering at a road map he had brought in from the car. "The problem with this state is that none of the roads go straight. Look at this." He held up the map, as if Daniel wasn't already intimately familiar with the spider web of cow paths and deer trails that made up Massachusetts roadways. "Disorganized."

"Can't argue with that."

"I don't think you should drive much more," Alex said.

"It's still four hours back to New York, and that's only if the traffic magically disappears. If we take roads that avoid Providence, that'll add at least another hour to the trip."

"How far is it to your father's house? That's what you usually do, isn't it? You take the train to and from Hartford, and only drive from there to Cape Cod. We could do that. Would there be a train into the city this afternoon?"

"It's two hours to Hartford. Maybe three. And then another two hours on the train."

"Would your father be able to meet us at the station to get the car?"

"I'm sure he would." Suddenly, everything seemed manageable. Daniel had been dreading the prospect of spending a limitless period of time stuck in a car that wasn't going anywhere. Somehow, driving out of his way to go to Hartford and then taking a nice predictable train seemed better, even if it didn't save them any time, because at least they wouldn't be stuck.

"You might as well come straight here and then we'll drive

you to the station," his father said when Daniel called him from the pay phone inside the restaurant. "Spare yourself the extra few miles, and we'll give you a drink."

Daniel's gut response was an adolescent urge to object, to insist that he didn't want to visit his dad, but honestly a drink and some air conditioning sounded great, and Alex would probably agree.

"Now you'll show me the pretty town," Alex said when Daniel hung up. "We'll go for a little walk. You can tell me all about the poor whales."

That was when it occurred to Daniel that he was being... managed, maybe. And that he had been since they turned off the highway. He didn't know why it annoyed him, since, honestly, he kind of managed Alex every day, taking a little extra care to make sure Alex could sidestep the things he found overwhelming and point him toward the things he liked best. It wasn't a burden, it was just, as far as Daniel cared, a basic part of friendship. He liked to look after his friends; he liked to make them happy. It was probably stupid for him to feel like Alex shouldn't do the same for him, but he was in a stupid kind of mood.

And, anyway, it *was* a pretty little town, and Alex was awfully pretty in it, so it wasn't exactly a hardship to go for a walk. It wasn't like Daniel ever forgot what Alex looked like, but in a different context, in the bright clear light reflecting off the water, water the exact gray-blue of Alex's eyes, it was hard to think of anything else.

Chapter Eight

Sometimes Alex forgot how Daniel acted when he was on edge. He was like a child, tapping his foot, biting his nails, pulling loose strings on the cuff of his shirt. Alex did not, professionally speaking, approve of marijuana, but he wondered if Daniel had one of his messily rolled joints packed away in his bag, because at this point it would be almost medicinal.

He seemed less antsy when they got back in the car, and Alex didn't know if that was because of the walk they had taken—Daniel seemed to need a certain amount of exercise just to avoid crawling out of own skin—or because he knew he wasn't going to be trapped in a car indefinitely.

The traffic on the road to Hartford was still pretty heavy but at least it moved steadily along, and when Daniel started changing lanes perhaps a bit more enthusiastically and frequently than warranted, Alex kept his mouth shut. When they pulled into Daniel's father's driveway late in the afternoon, Daniel sighed with relief.

It was a pretty house, almost like a miniature version of Daniel's grandmother's house, although Alex thought he probably shouldn't mention that. He knew Daniel hadn't grown up here, and that Daniel's father had only moved here ten or so years ago, but Daniel didn't knock on the door, just pushed it open and immediately dropped to the floor to greet the large, shaggy dog who bounded over.

"Oh, leave him alone, Stella. Have some manners." That was Everett, who was attempting to get a hold of the dog's collar. "Or at least let them into the house."

The dog looked like she had no intention of letting anyone into the house until she had been thoroughly petted. Alex stood there, awkwardly holding his suitcase and letting the dog sniff his shoes. He waved tentatively at Everett.

"Hi, Alex. Traffic must have been unbearable if it took you this long. Daniel, you look like hell. Alex, you look—well, you never look like hell but you look like you could use a stiff drink."

As if on cue, Tom walked in with a pitcher. "Good to see both of—oh Jesus, you do look awful, Dan. The last train's at six and you'll catch it if we leave in the next half hour. But do you want to spend the night instead?"

Alex did not want to spend the night. One night away from home was more than enough, thank you very much. Two days of dealing with strange places and attempting to be social was about 1.75 days too many. On the other hand, he was exhausted, and the idea of not being able to close his eyes for the duration of a train trip and then however long it took to get home from the train station sounded almost as bad. And Daniel really did look frazzled.

"Go away so we can figure out what to do," Daniel said, after hugging his father and Everett.

"It's up to you," Alex said when they were alone. He didn't add *I'm unhappy either way* because he didn't think that would help, and besides, he suspected Daniel already knew.

"The train would get us into the city at around eight," Daniel said.

Alex didn't doubt for a minute that Daniel would catch the train if Alex asked him to, and that made it a lot easier to agree to stay. "We should stay. I'm about ready to pass out, anyway."

"Then I'm going to pour half the contents of that pitcher down my throat. Do you want to lie down? I can show you where the guest room is."

"In a bit," Alex said. "First we drink."

He didn't know if Daniel had said something to his father and Everett, but nobody tried to talk to him, just left him in peace with a glass of what turned out to be a whiskey sour that was mostly whiskey. They sat outside while the dog alternately got confused by butterflies and allowed herself to be doted on. Alex had seen Daniel be ridiculous with dogs and it was the opposite of a surprise that his father was the same way. At dinner, Alex watched Everett sigh and pretend not to notice every time Tom slipped a morsel of food to the dog.

He knew that he probably ought to go lie down, because he was running out of patience with himself, other people, and the entire weekend, but he didn't want to move. Besides, it was still light out, and if he fell asleep now, he'd wake up at the crack of dawn tomorrow and have to tiptoe around a strange house. Instead, he let the porch swing lull him into a stupor while he listened to Daniel get mocked by his father for some bad opinion he had about some or another sport. When he shut his eyes, he was aware of the smell of Daniel's shampoo.

"Let's get you to bed," Daniel said from very nearby.

"It's still early."

"Not for you, it isn't. Come on."

"The bed in the spare room is already made up," said Tom.

"And the sofa in the den pulls out, if you want. You know where the linens are, Dan, right?"

Alex was dimly aware of Daniel carrying both their bags upstairs and ushering him into a room that was mercifully cool, then planting a quick peck on his cheek before shutting the door.

* * *

Daniel was trying to lure Stella to sleep with him on the sofa bed, but the dog persisted in lying on the floor and smiling up at him while wagging her tail.

"Everett's spent years training her not to go on the furniture, and if you ruin it, I'll be the one with hell to pay," his father complained from the doorway. "If you don't want to sleep alone, you should go up and—"

"Don't even finish that sentence," Daniel warned.

"He fell asleep with his head on your shoulder," his father said. "Dan."

"I don't think he even realized he was doing it." Daniel yawned.

"Go to sleep, kid. You look like you need it."

Daniel said goodnight to his father and shut the lights, but before going to bed he wanted to check on Alex, just to make sure he hadn't fallen asleep on the floor or fully dressed or something. He had seemed pretty out of it. As quietly as he could, Daniel pushed the door open and saw Alex fast asleep in bed, under the covers, safe and sound.

Right when he was about to shut the door, Stella pushed her way in and stuck her nose in Alex's face.

"Stella, no," Daniel whispered.

Alex's eyes flew open.

"It's just the dog. And me," Daniel whispered. "Go back to sleep."

Alex mumbled something in Ukrainian to the dog and patted the bed, and the little traitor hopped right up, settling beside Alex and giving Daniel an unmistakably smug look. "You speak Ukrainian now?" he asked Stella. "Is that the trick?" And then, to Alex, "I thought you didn't like dogs."

"Why did you think that?" Alex asked sleepily, and then said something else to the dog, fond and low, again in Ukrainian.

Daniel wasn't sure why he thought that, actually. Probably because Alex always seemed to withdraw a little when dogs were around. It wasn't such a leap to conclude that dogs were too much for him.

"Had a dog that looked like this when I was little," Alex said. And then Daniel didn't need to ask about the rest, because for Alex, "when I was little" meant before New York, and it also meant he wasn't going to talk about it. What Daniel knew, he mainly knew from Alex's parents, and they didn't say much about it either. But he bet that if he asked Mrs. Savchenko, she'd tell him that they had to leave a dog behind at some point. Christ.

When Daniel thought about Alex's early childhood—from what he gathered, it started with bombs and was one string of evacuations and expulsions until they arrived in New York—it didn't seem any kind of surprise that he sought out the comfort of a routine, and that only made it more of a pleasure to help him have that.

Daniel watched Alex scratch the dog's ears. "Are you going to let her sleep in your bed?"

"Absolutely not. I don't like dogs that much," Alex said,

nudging the dog so she hopped back off the bed and curled up on the floor as if that had been her plan all along. "And there wouldn't be room for you, then."

Daniel had to pause to make sure he understood that. "You don't have to share. I made up the sofa bed for myself."

Alex held up a corner of the covers. "Get in?"

It was too dark for Daniel to see Alex's face but he did as he was told, climbing between sheets that were already warm from Alex's body, his heart beating a little too hard, his cheeks a little too hot. It was just a bed, it was just Alex.

"Are we sleeping, or—"

Alex kissed him before Daniel finished the sentence. Well, kiss might be overstating it: he pressed his lips against Daniel's and froze, as if that was as far as his planning took him. Or maybe as if the idea of kissing Daniel seemed fine in theory but awkward in practice. Or maybe just like he had run out of courage.

Well, that was fine because Daniel, at the moment, had enough courage for the both of them. He'd been wanting to touch Alex forever and he didn't know if he'd get another chance, and—maybe more importantly—he knew he was good at this part. So he tucked his body against Alex's and kissed him back. He wanted to take his time, here, wanted to give Alex a chance to get used to the two of them like this, but also give him a chance to decide he didn't want this at all. He'd rather stop now than find out later that Alex had regrets. He'd choose the smaller, sooner heartbreak.

He tried to keep it slow, keep it gentle, like maybe if he didn't move too quickly he might be able to convince Alex that this wasn't so different from when they cuddled on the sofa. With his hand cupping Alex's jaw, he could feel Alex's pulse fluttering beneath his fingertips.

"This all right?" Daniel asked, barely moving his mouth away from Alex's as he spoke. Alex's only answer was to wrap an arm around Daniel's back and haul him closer so Daniel was half on top of him. And that—that really worked for Daniel, both being pressed close to Alex and being manhandled a little. They were both only wearing pajama bottoms and T-shirts and it really didn't feel anything like cuddling on the sofa anymore.

"This feel good?" Daniel asked, even though it was pretty obvious that it did. He just wanted to hear it.

"Daniel," Alex said. "It feels good." He slid a hand under Daniel's shirt, palm flat against his back, and then the other hand followed, searching for skin. Daniel took the hint and pulled his shirt off and Alex went still, just looking, as if he hadn't seen Daniel without his shirt a dozen times or more—when the water got turned off in Daniel's apartment and he needed to shower at Alex's, or whenever Alex stopped by and scolded Daniel for gardening without a shirt and scandalizing the neighborhood. There wasn't anything new for Alex to be looking at like that, and even if there were, Daniel had a mirror in his apartment and eyes in his head and he knew that there wasn't anything *that* interesting happening under his clothes.

But Alex didn't seem to know any of this, because he looked transfixed as he skimmed his hands down Daniel's sides, a thumb taking a detour to touch a nipple, and then doing it again when Daniel made a sound. "Does that feel good?" Alex asked, a little teasing.

"Yeah," Daniel breathed, too earnest, too fast. He slid a leg between Alex's, only partly as payback, then caught Alex's moan with his own mouth.

Alex was hard against his thigh now. Daniel slid a hand to his hip. "Will you let me take care of you?" A shudder ran through Alex—whether at the words, or the idea, or the feel of Daniel against him, Daniel couldn't tell.

"We shouldn't. Not here," Alex said finally.

"Okay," Daniel started to pull away, but Alex held him in place.

"I don't want to worry about making noise," Alex said, and yes, that was reasonable, and probably something Daniel should have thought of himself.

"Do you want me to go sleep on the sofa?"

"No," Alex said. "I don't want to stop." He pushed a piece of hair behind Daniel's ear.

"Okay." So Daniel kissed him again, and kissed him some more, until he felt Alex go lax beneath him, until they were breathing together more than kissing, and then Daniel fell asleep too.

* * *

When Alex woke up he registered Daniel's body half across his own before he even remembered where he was or how they had gotten that way. He should have known that given half a chance, Daniel would sleep like a baby koala, managing to cling to Alex with both arms despite being fast asleep. It shouldn't be endearing, not when it had woken Alex up at—he reached for his watch—well, six wasn't such a bad time to wake up, he supposed.

And this wasn't a bad way to wake up, either, Daniel warm and heavy, his breath steady and soft against Alex's neck. Last night had been—well, if he had been more alert, he might not have asked Daniel to get into bed. But he had spent two entire days with Daniel rarely out of arm's reach and somehow it wasn't enough. He had wanted more, had wanted Daniel closer, had wanted all the things he tried so hard not to want. But maybe he didn't need to try so hard; maybe he could let himself want, at least a little, because Daniel wanted some of those things too.

He gave himself a minute to remember Daniel last night, the way his mouth had been eager and gentle at once, the way he had held Alex's face as if—as if nothing, Alex told himself firmly. That was just how Daniel probably was with everyone he got into bed with.

He wondered how to extricate himself without waking Daniel, then remembered that Daniel routinely slept through police sirens and fire alarms, and just got out of bed. Sure enough, Daniel's eyelids didn't even flutter.

Alex made sure he was decent and went downstairs. The kitchen was empty and quiet, despite the presence of a full pot of coffee. He decided not to think too hard about it and just poured himself a mug and sat at the table.

A few minutes later, Everett appeared in the kitchen.

"Sleep okay?" Everett asked, pouring his own coffee.

"Yes, thank you." Alex liked Everett. He was quiet and didn't seem to expect Alex to be anything other than quiet himself, which paradoxically made it easier for Alex to say the right things. "Thank you for letting me stay. I was so tired last night."

"I wish I knew why spending time in a car is so exhausting. You're just sitting there. It ought to be relaxing. Daniel still asleep?"

Of course, as soon as Everett came downstairs and saw that

nobody was asleep on the sofa, he would have known that Alex and Daniel had shared a bed. Alex tried not to feel self-conscious. He was thirty years old. Everett himself lived with Daniel's father. And Everett didn't even seem curious about where anyone had slept; he was just making polite conversation.

"Daniel's basically in a coma," Alex said.

"He's been like that since he was a teenager. Tommy's not much better. Here, let me top off your coffee." He took Alex's cup, and while he was fiddling with the coffee maker, his back to Alex, said, "Tommy's been getting up as soon as the newspaper hits the front door, these days, though. He checks the headlines, turns the coffee maker on for me, and goes back to bed."

Daniel had also started obsessively checking headlines that spring. The president—or at least some people who worked for him—were involved in some very boring crimes that Alex knew he ought to care about. He didn't know if it was some innate Eastern European expectation that leaders were up to no good, but he found that he was more surprised that Americans were surprised by all this than he was by the actual conspiracy that was being revealed in hearings and interviews. There was something so optimistic about expecting people to follow the rules, just like there was something optimistic about expecting your government not to send you off to be killed in a war for no good reason.

He didn't mention any of this to Daniel. Probably expecting your leaders not to be criminals and not to send people to unnecessary deaths was a good thing.

"He thinks the world of you, you know," Everett said, sitting back down. "No, you don't need to say anything. Just listen to an old man for a moment." He slid a full cup of black coffee in front of Alex before Alex could decide whether he was supposed to insist that Everett wasn't old. "Tommy's convinced the two of you are together and it's really only a matter of time before either he or Patty says something that'll send you running for the hills, so brace yourself."

"Patricia says things all the time," Alex lamented. She never came right out with the sort of assumption that would make Alex twitchy, instead camping out on the line between delicate innuendo and plausible deniability. Alex was pretty sure the only reason it didn't send him into a snit was that she never put him in a position where he had to say anything.

"I guess what I mean is that—Christ, this is awkward. I'm no good at this. When Daniel came home two years ago, he was out of sorts. He was furious with his mother for making sure he got sent someplace that wasn't Vietnam, probably furious with himself for being relieved about it, and furious at the world for having let the war happen in the first place."

Alex hadn't realized that Patricia had done something to ensure that her son wasn't sent to Vietnam, but it made sense. Rich people had connections, and he wasn't going to fault anyone for trying to save their child—but he also wasn't going to think about how that probably meant somebody else's child had to go instead. Daniel had probably thought enough about that already.

"Anyway," Everett went on, "he isn't good at being angry. He was such an even-keeled kid. When you met him, he was still angry, and I wonder if you had the impression that he was tougher than he is."

"I've never once been under the impression that Daniel is tough," Alex said honestly, which made Everett laugh even though it wasn't a joke. But it was true. Daniel was the opposite of tough, and maybe that was partly due to how sheltered he had always been, but the rest was just because he had a soft heart.

"I guess what I'm saying is that he doesn't know how to protect himself. He says what he means. So if he tells you something, you probably ought to believe it."

Alex didn't know why he was being told this. Daniel's willingness to say what he meant was one of the things Alex liked best about him. And of course Alex would believe him. Case in point: Daniel had said that he and Alex could have sex, that it didn't have to be a big deal. Alex would keep that in mind instead of letting his imagination take over, instead of replaying the events of last night again and again, searching for meaning that wasn't there.

So he thanked Everett for the advice, because that was the polite thing to do, and excused himself to take a shower.

Chapter Nine

Alex was ragged by the time they got off the subway on Sunday afternoon. He needed to be at work in the morning; before that, he needed to spend as long as possible in absolute silence, alone, undisturbed by anyone or anything.

"Option one or option two?" Daniel asked cheerfully. "One is that I come over and make you dinner. Two is that you go home alone and enjoy peace and quiet."

"Two," Alex said, probably too curtly. "I mean, I need to be alone. I'm dying over here. It's not you."

Daniel laughed. "I didn't think it was. Will I see you tomorrow, or Tuesday, or should I wait to hear from you?"

"Tuesday," Alex said immediately. He'd still want an empty apartment tomorrow after work.

"Okay." Daniel kissed him on the cheek, just a quick nothing of a peck, exactly the same as Alex had seen him give Mary or one of his other friends and yet not something he had ever done to Alex. Alex stood frozen still, not sure whether he was supposed to do something, say something, and then Daniel left.

Alex unlocked the door to his building and went upstairs,

almost delirious with relief when he let himself into his apartment and saw everything where it belonged, as if two nights away might somehow be enough for his home to forget how it was supposed to be. Which, obviously, made no sense but Alex was pretty sure he wasn't capable of sense at the moment. He took a shower and went to sleep, not bothering with dinner.

When he woke up, he was relieved to remember that it was Monday morning—he had always been relieved by Mondays, and had long since learned not to mention this to normal people, who thought, probably correctly, that there was something wrong with anyone who was relieved to return to school or work, even on days when school or work held no particular thrills.

It was the routine that Alex liked, the predictability. Even though his days didn't resemble one another in the specifics—there was enough variety among the reasons why kids from birth to adolescence might need to visit a doctor to keep him on his toes—the shape of his days remained the same. See a patient, figure out what they needed, fill out paperwork, do it again.

"How was Cape Cod?" Mary asked as they ate lunch in her office. Alex couldn't stand the smell of food in his own office and—Christ, he was impossible.

"Fine," Alex said.

"Nice to get out of the city?"

"Not really." Alex never particularly wanted to get out of the city. It had been interesting, he supposed, to see something new. He had enjoyed the beach, that much was true. Spending time with Daniel had been good until it wasn't.

"Okay," Mary said dubiously, her eyebrows raised. "Everything all right?"

Alex ran his fingernail across the place where his chopsticks had broken apart unevenly. "Why wouldn't it be?"

"Everything okay with Daniel?"

He didn't answer right away, which probably said as much as any answer could.

"He didn't bring lunch," Mary pointed out, which obviously they both already knew since they were eating dumplings that had just been delivered. "He usually brings lunch on Monday."

"I asked him to stay away for a few days."

"Again?"

"Look, I already feel shitty about it. But I had to talk to people all weekend and I can't do it anymore."

"You're talking to me," Mary said. Apparently she was only going to state the obvious today.

Alex bit his tongue before he could say "not by choice" or something equally rude, but honestly, Mary didn't really count as people. It was easy to be around her. She annoyed him sometimes, and he annoyed her, but he was used to all the ways she got on his nerves. It took almost no effort to be around her.

It usually didn't take any effort to be around Daniel, either. He slotted himself into Alex's life so easily that Alex felt guilty for not noticing the things Daniel was doing to accommodate him. "Does it take a lot of effort for you to placate me?" Alex asked.

Mary put her chopsticks down. "What do you mean?"

"For example, we're eating in your office because I don't like food in mine. And when I'm crabby and don't want to talk after work, you always leave me alone. You never play music when we're balancing the books, even though I know you prefer to work with music on. And you always make plans with me two days in advance because I hate short notice."

"Is this about when I told you to stop being so difficult? Because I felt shitty as soon as I said it."

"No, it's—well, yes, that's part of it. But I really am difficult, and I'd say that I don't want to be but—"

"You aren't difficult."

He gave her a skeptical look. Usually she didn't bother with polite half-truths.

"Okay, let me put it another way," Mary said. "You're a great doctor and a good listener and you'd do anything to help someone in need. If I needed something, you'd make sure I had it. So why wouldn't I do the same to you?"

Alex couldn't think of anything Mary had ever needed from him, but he was afraid to point this out in case it caused her to realize that he was a useless friend.

"Okay, let's talk about someone else being difficult," Mary said. "I love Paul, right? He can't do laundry, and I can't figure out if he's just a secret imbecile about this one thing or if he's deliberately being lazy so I'll do it myself. So instead of thinking about it, I send our clothes out to be washed. Also, he thinks his mother is a saint and she is really fucking not. He could spend another day every month with me if he weren't totally spineless with his boss, but instead—anyway, I could go on for the rest of the day but you get the picture, and we both have one o'clock appointments. I love him more than I love anyone, but he isn't perfect and neither am I. He probably has a similar list of things he doesn't love about me."

Alex strongly doubted that. He had seen the way Paul looked at Mary.

That evening, he went home and ate some mediocre defrosted pierogi for dinner in front of the television and debated calling Daniel. He might have overestimated in thinking he'd need two days of peace and quiet, and he also knew that if he asked Daniel to come over and not talk, Daniel would do it. That only made him feel worse, that he could ask for something both rude and ridiculous and Daniel would give it to him without question.

That night in the shower he thought about Daniel kissing him, Daniel braced on one arm above him in bed. It had only been kissing, and there was no logical reason why it had him this worked up. He didn't think he had ever been kissed quite that—nicely, maybe? Was *nice* even a word that could be applied to something that had made them both undeniably hard?

He was thirty years old and hardly inexperienced, but the memory of Daniel's lips on his, the way Daniel had asked to take care of him—Christ—those words kept replaying in his head. He had said it like that was what he really wanted, more than anything, and Alex believed him. Daniel had told him it was nicer with a friend. Maybe that's how it always with Daniel.

It bothered Alex; it bothered him more than he wanted to think about, that what for him had been an unprecedentedly lovely half hour was, for Daniel, just the sort of thing that he *did.* And then Alex felt even worse—not just petty and mean but actively stupid—when he realized that he could have had more if only he hadn't sent Daniel away the previous day. He could have asked Daniel upstairs, could have had more kisses, more of Daniel's callused hands and infuriating patience, if only Alex had been—well, if only Alex had been an entirely different person.

That was an old and familiar line of self-criticism, though, and one that Alex thought he had given up for good. He was used to certain things simply not being for him, but usually these were things he had no interest in, anyway. For weeks, though—ever since that night at dinner with Mary and Paul—Alex had found himself wishing he were someone else, someone who could be something to Daniel that Alex could never be.

He couldn't think like that. He knew from experience that this was the kind of thinking that ate away at you, that chewed up whatever happiness you had managed to find.

He felt guilty as he wrapped a hand around himself, like he shouldn't be jerking off to the memory of someone whose actual presence he had refused. Not guilty enough to stop, though, but he did manage not to say Daniel's name out loud, so maybe he could pretend it hadn't happened.

* * *

Daniel had a deadline, but it was a week away and therefore not worth thinking about, so he weeded the garden—it was amazing how many weeds popped up in the span of a warm weekend. Then he fussed with the placement of a few stones in what was shaping up to be a pretty decent pathway. When it got too hot to work comfortably outside, he sat with his back against the rough brick wall of his building, surveying the garden.

He was starting to think of this as his project. It was a community garden, obviously, and it hadn't even been his idea. He had done most of the physical labor, but he had only done what he was told. He hadn't known anything about gardening when he started, and knew only marginally more now. What he had learned was the most efficient way to break up dirt, how to make a sieve that would filter out rocks, glass, and nails, and how to build a garden bed so that rain wouldn't wash away the dirt.

He had also learned that "am I being detained, officer?" was what you said when cops wanted to know if you had a permit to build on the land you were gardening. He had learned, too, how to go to the city records office and find out which vacant lots, formerly occupied by demolished tenements, had been forfeited to the city when the owners defaulted on their loans. He also learned that this was one of those properties, and that there were twenty others in a five-block radius of his building, some adjacent to one another, which were tempting locations for a larger garden.

This garden was nearly—well, not done, because he was starting to understand that a garden was never done, but ready to be left alone for people to enjoy. Daniel could take his shovels and pickax and paucity of accumulated knowledge a few blocks over and repeat the process in another empty lot. He wasn't the only one with that idea—there was an empty lot near Alex's clinic that someone had strewn with wildflower seeds, and a space off Fifth Street where some people had gotten together and planted vegetables.

He could do that; he knew he could. But it wasn't a career, it wasn't what people meant when they talked about doing something with your life. What he didn't know was whether that mattered. He had a job, one he liked, and which paid his bills as long as he didn't have much in the way of bills—which he didn't. But the actual writing part of his job took maybe ten hours a week, except for those few times a year he traveled to profile an artist or cover a festival. He was twenty-six and should be doing something with his life that wasn't dicking around for free in a garden that didn't even belong to him.

"Jesus Christ," Blanca said when Daniel told her as much later that afternoon in her and Miriam's apartment. "Are you complaining about earning too much money for too little work?"

"I—" Daniel started.

"No. No more talking until half this joint is gone."

"I went to a very fancy school," Daniel said later, lying on Blanca's kilim rug and staring at the ceiling. "And a fancy college. I should probably do something with it? That's all I'm saying. You're a teacher. Alex is a doctor. Miriam's going to be a lawyer. These are all..." He waved the joint in the air, briefly distracted by a curl of smoke. "Real jobs. And all the people who are dead probably wish they had real jobs?" No, that didn't come out right. "I feel like I should do something real because not everybody had a chance."

Blanca made a jerking-off motion and Daniel started to laugh.

"The government had people murdered, but not you, so you think you need a real job? You're dumb." She took the joint away from him. "Fancy schools didn't stop you from being dumb."

Daniel laughed some more, even though Blanca was very rude and somebody ought to tell her so.

He was pretty sure he had used up his allotment of talking about himself for the afternoon, and so he changed the record and listen to Blanca complain about how Miriam wouldn't eat meat anymore and instead wanted them to have things like millet. Daniel hadn't known it was possible to have that many feelings about millet.

When Miriam got home she made dinner and it really was terrible, filled with ominously crunchy things, and he kept catching Blanca's eye and having to bite his tongue so he didn't laugh. Eventually he fell asleep on their sofa, happy and vaguely stoned and a little sunburned.

When he went back to his own apartment, he thought about calling Alex, but Alex had said he needed until tomorrow, which was—it was fine. Daniel had had a good day. He had never been clingy with friends or lovers—well, not emotionally clingy, at least. He was pretty sure he was physically clingy to anyone who would let him.

Sometimes Alex needed time to himself. A few weeks ago Blanca had literally pushed Daniel out of her apartment and told him to breathe his own oxygen for a change, and it hadn't even bothered him. He liked when people told him what they needed.

A little, annoying voice inside him that sounded a lot like his mother asked if he was being honest about what *he* needed, and Daniel decided to ignore that voice. Alex hadn't done anything he hadn't already done a dozen times before. The fact they had fooled around did change things, but not in any way Daniel could articulate. Possibly because "fooled around" seemed so inaccurate as to be dishonest. Possibly because Daniel knew that everything he felt for Alex made fooling around with him the dumbest idea he'd had in a long while.

And that was a depressing thought, so he got changed and went to hear a band he had been meaning to check out, and by the time he was walking home, he only went a little out of his way to go past Alex's building, only glanced up for a few seconds to look at a dark window.

Chapter Ten

Alex probably shouldn't have been surprised to find Daniel sitting in the waiting room after his last patient left, but he was surprised to see that Daniel didn't have any food with him. When Daniel stopped by after work, he usually brought take out to share with Mary.

"I wasn't sure whether you'd want Monday food or Tuesday food," Daniel explained. "I thought maybe your week got thrown off by being away over the weekend, so I figured I'd check."

And, okay, Alex had a food schedule. Of course he did; he had a schedule for a lot of things. But nobody was supposed to actually *know* that Alex had a food schedule.

"It's just that usually on Mondays I come by your apartment and either I cook or we eat whatever's in your fridge," Daniel went on. "But on Tuesday I pick up take-out and bring it here." A smile broke out over his face. "Wait, did you think it was a coincidence that I always show up at the same times with the same food?"

Alex must have been staring, because Daniel looked away and scuffed the toe of his boot on the linoleum. "Or I could go and catch up with you later in the week? Maybe I was presumptuous in thinking—"

"I have to go to the grocery store," Alex said. Usually he did his errands on Saturday, but this Saturday he had been away, so now his refrigerator had nothing but some apples, three eggs, and a stick of margarine he had bought months ago and decided was too disgusting to eat but couldn't bring himself to throw out. "Can we get groceries and I'll make something?"

Alex hoped Daniel appreciated exactly how bold and daring he was being in going to the grocery store on Tuesday rather than Saturday. It was like fucking Mardi Gras over here, everything upside down.

They went to the grocery store, but Alex's mind was too scrambled to remember what he needed to buy. He was afraid of winding up with nothing but cabbage and lunch meat if he had to make any choices, so he trailed along behind Daniel, holding the basket.

Daniel's hair was still wet, like he had stepped out of the shower right before coming to see Alex. Six p.m. was an objectively insane time of day to take a shower, but Daniel's hair curled where he tucked it behind his ears and where it skimmed the collar of his T-shirt. He hadn't shaved, but it looked like maybe he had yesterday. There was no discernible pattern to when or whether Daniel shaved. Sometimes he'd go entire weeks relatively clean-shaven and other times he looked like he was going to throw in the towel and grow a beard. Usually he just looked scruffy, and Alex was sure he shouldn't find it so appealing.

Alex had spent a long time trying not to find anything physically appealing about Daniel, but after they'd kissed, it seemed a waste of energy to pretend he didn't find Daniel attractive. It was only rational to acknowledge that he liked the look of Daniel's ass in those jeans, the way his shoulders stretched his T-shirt. Now Alex was standing in front of the coffee beans at the A&P thinking about kissing Daniel, and that wouldn't do.

When they got inside Alex's apartment, Daniel shoved the entire paper sack of groceries into Alex's refrigerator and kissed him, as if he had been reading Alex's mind, or maybe because he had just been thinking about the same thing all along. Alex's hands went automatically to Daniel's hips, curving around them, a thumb slipping into the belt loop of his jeans.

Alex wanted—he wanted to make sense of this, and those kisses on Saturday night hadn't made sense. He deepened the kiss, trying to get it on familiar ground, and felt Daniel's fingers grip the collar of his shirt, keeping him close. When Alex touched the tip of his tongue to the seam of Daniel's lips, Daniel made a needy sound, met him halfway.

This was the kind of kiss that was the prelude to more, and Alex knew this terrain. He slid his hand under Daniel's shirt, fingertips skimming beneath the waistband of his jeans as he buried his face in Daniel's neck.

The couch was right there. The wall was even closer. They probably didn't need either, or at least Alex didn't.

"Slow down," Daniel said, which was the last thing in the world Alex wanted to do.

"Why?" Alex asked, speaking the word into the soft skin of Daniel's neck.

"Because otherwise I'm going to go off in thirty seconds and it'll be embarrassing?"

Alex laughed, and he wasn't supposed to be laughing. He was back on unfamiliar ground, a place where he didn't have a map.

"Okay," Alex said, because what else could he say? He pulled back to look at Daniel and was pleased to see that he was flushed, his lips wet and pink. He resisted the urge to tuck a loose strand of hair behind Daniel's ear, unsure why this urge seemed so important to resist. "What do you want?"

"I...don't really care, I guess? I mean, if you're asking about particulars, that is. Broadly speaking, I'd like to get into your bed. What happens there is—well, I'm easy to please."

Alex maybe could have guessed as much, if he had let himself wonder what Daniel would be like in bed, what he'd want, what he'd ask for. But he hadn't. He very carefully had not let his mind wander anywhere even in the neighborhood of that topic, and so now the image of Daniel, in his bed, being easily pleased, being game for whatever Alex asked for, short-circuited something in his brain.

"Okay. Bed, then," Alex said, because that was the one thing he could do something about without risk of blacking out or saying something mortifying.

Alex's bed was made, white bedspread pulled over white sheets, everything clean and tidy the way it always was. Daniel had been here dozens if not hundreds of times already, would probably not even have noticed if the entire contents of Alex's dresser had been dumped all over the bed and floor, but still Alex was stupidly relieved to see that everything was the way it ought to be.

Alex sat on the edge of the bed, which seemed a safe enough choice until Daniel came over and straddled his lap, and Alex went right back to being overwhelmed.

If he asked Daniel to just—to take care of him, like he had offered, whatever that even meant—he'd do it, Alex knew. And then Alex wouldn't have to make any decisions. He could just look, and touch, and feel. But when he opened his mouth to say something, he couldn't find the words.

"Let's get some clothes off," Daniel murmured into his ear, and that was an easy yes, the clothes obviously had to go, Daniel's clothes most of all, so that was what Alex set about trying to make happen. He worked open Daniel's belt buckle, then undid the buttons on Daniel's jeans with unaccountably shaky fingers. He watched, dry-mouthed, as Daniel tugged off his T-shirt. And before he knew it, Daniel had Alex's shirt off, had him stripped to the waist.

"God. Look at you," Daniel said. "Can I take your pants off?"

"Yeah," Alex said, instead of *yes please I think I'll cry if you don't*, so that had to be a victory, even though his voice was already rough.

Usually Alex didn't particularly want to be the only one naked, honestly preferred to remove only key articles of clothing, but the way Daniel was looking at him made him want to either stay naked for the rest of his life or immediately hide under the bedspread. He couldn't quite decide. They hadn't turned any lights on, but the sun hadn't set and the room was bright enough that Alex knew he was on full display. He could feel his face heat, could feel the flush spread down his neck and chest, and he did the only thing that seemed possible, which was to grab Daniel's hand and tug him down to the mattress with him.

"Too much?" Daniel asked, and Alex didn't know if he was asking if the sex aspect was too much—which, no—or whether he was overwhelmed—which, definitely, but it wasn't going to stop him.

"No," Alex said. "It's good."

"Tell me what you want."

Alex didn't know where to start. He didn't know, period. Look—he knew what he liked. And he also knew what he felt comfortable doing. The Venn diagram of those two things had a big enough overlap that it wasn't a problem, even if it did lead to a certain amount of repetition. Not that repetition was a bad thing, when you were repeating things that you liked.

"I—your mouth," Alex said, because apparently he couldn't get any more explicit than that right now. Daniel kissed his jaw, his neck, his chest, obviously working his way down, and Alex felt the tension ratchet up inside him.

He didn't usually like to be fussed over—didn't need it, he was already hard, it was a waste of time—but he kept watching the fall of Daniel's hair over his own chest, noticing the strands that the sun had lightened almost to blond. His arms and shoulders were tan, and while Alex already knew that it had been some time since Daniel had been the skinny kid he met outside a seedy club, he hadn't let himself pay detailed attention to what exactly had happened in the meantime. His biceps were thick, his shoulders broad. Shoveling, he thought inanely. More men should shovel things.

When Daniel closed his lips around the head of Alex's erection, Alex had to bite his fist to stop himself from making a sound. Daniel pulled off—terrible, why—and started stroking him with a loose fist. "I want to hear you," he said, before sucking him down. When Alex groaned, Daniel made a sound around him that vibrated through his dick, and fine, sounds were great, Alex could keep doing that.

He was going slow (inefficient, Alex couldn't help but think, although it was clear even to him that that Daniel wasn't going for efficiency, not in the least), a drawn-out tease of a blowjob, flicking the underside of Alex's dick with his tongue and keeping his fist lazy and loose on Alex's shaft. Alex's hips twitched, wanting more, but he forced himself to stay still.

When Daniel took hold of Alex's hand, Alex immediately twined his fingers in Daniel's although he couldn't have said why, handholding not usually—or ever—factoring into blowjobs, in his experience. But then Daniel squeezed his hand once before placing it on the back of his head.

And that meant—well, it usually meant one thing. Ordinarily, Alex would thrust up a bit, see if that was okay, and then proceed accordingly. But it was one thing to misread a signal in the bathroom at a bar and then have to apologize for attempting to fuck someone's face, but it was another thing entirely to accidentally choke your closest friend and then have him make you dinner in your own kitchen. So Alex remained agonizingly still, contenting himself with petting Daniel's hair stupidly, the silky strands slipping through his fingers, then getting distracted by the pretty curve of his ear.

Only when Daniel gripped Alex's hips and tugged did Alex finally allow himself to take the hint. He thrust up, just a little, and was rewarded with a moan and the impossible heat of Daniel's throat. And—God—the clench of Daniel's fingers on his hips, the hot slide of his tongue, the way his hair landed on Alex's belly. He wasn't going to last—and maybe that was for the best, because it was too much, too good.

"Daniel. I'm going to—you're making me—" Alex made an extremely halfhearted attempt to shove at Daniel's shoulder and wasn't surprised in the least when Daniel didn't pull off, when instead he let Alex come down his throat.

Alex could hardly feel his legs. He knew he had an arm flung over his eyes but didn't have the energy to move it. "I'll do you," he mumbled, waving in the general direction of the bottom of the bed.

Daniel laughed. "Yeah, no. You just lie there and let me make a mess of you? Or, wait, no, you probably hate—"

"Do it," Alex said, moving his arm away from his eyes so he could watch. And he was glad he did. Daniel made a picture like that, straddling Alex's thighs, his jeans around his hips and his cock in his fist, his gaze hot on Alex as he moved his hand.

Alex paid attention to the way Daniel touched himself, to the hitch in his breath as he got close, to the way the muscles of his arm bunched and rippled as he moved. He had a tube of KY Jelly in the nightstand and should probably offer it, but it looked like Daniel was doing just fine on his own, thumbing the moisture from the head of his cock and using that.

"You're gorgeous," Daniel said. "Perfect. Could look at you all—fuck, I'm going to—"

And, okay, Alex didn't actually *like* being covered in come, but he liked watching Daniel do it, he liked feeling it happen.

"Fuck," Daniel said, low and drawn out. "God." He reached for his own T-shirt, and before Alex could protest that he had a box of tissues right on the nightstand, cleaned up Alex's chest.

"Come here," Alex managed, not even knowing exactly what he wanted, other than Daniel to be closer. Daniel crawled up the bed, hesitating at the top. Alex pulled him into a kiss, tasting himself on him, which he had always thought was pretty gross and still thought was gross but he wanted to kiss Daniel anyway.

* * *

Daniel's strategy here was to play it cool, to act the same as he ever did, like maybe that way Alex wouldn't notice that anything out of the ordinary had happened.

Alex was still lying on the bed, his hair going every which way, his cheeks pink, completely naked. Daniel tried not to stare.

He forced himself onto his feet so he wouldn't be tempted to crawl into Alex's arms.

"I'm going to go make dinner," Daniel said. He pulled his jeans up but didn't bother with a shirt—his own was unwearable and Alex was in no condition to point him in the direction of a clean one.

"Wash your hands first," Alex mumbled. Daniel snorted, but made sure he washed his hands for long enough that Alex wouldn't have to think about germs.

He had bought bread, cheese, butter, and a can of tomato soup. Nothing fancy, because he had no interest in actually cooking tonight, and he had made so many grilled cheese sandwiches in his life that he was pretty sure he could make them even completely fucked out and delirious.

Not that he was either fucked out or delirious at the moment. They had just taken the edge off. At least, that was what Daniel hoped. He had spent the past few days—weeks, maybe even longer if he wanted to be honest with himself—with arousal and denial fighting to see who got the upper hand, and now that arousal had won a decisive victory, he really wasn't done yet.

But first, dinner. He moved easily around Alex's kitchen, having done more cooking here than he had anywhere else. Nothing that could realistically be described as cooking took place in Daniel's own apartment—there was only so much you could do with a hotplate, and he didn't want to find out what would happen if he tried to connect a stove to the gas in his apartment. He didn't even know if there was a functioning gas line into his apartment in the first place. Blanca and Miriam had a stove, but it had been there for decades, by the looks of it.

He washed the can opener after pouring the soup into a pot,

because that was what Alex always did. He didn't think he had ever seen his mother wash a can opener, but it wasn't like he was paying close attention. His father didn't use cans when cooking, which was his own ridiculous problem.

While he buttered the slices of bread, he realized Alex was still in the bedroom. Usually, when Daniel made dinner, Alex was in the kitchen with him, either helping or bossing him around or just talking. Daniel paused, a pat of too-cold butter still on his knife. Should he have gone home? Was this about to get awkward? No, that was absurd. They ate dinner at Alex's apartment a couple times a week. That wouldn't change because of one blowjob, would it?

He put the buttered bread in the skillet and listened to it sizzle, then layered on some sliced cheese. He was used to Alex needing time alone. He had just had this conversation with himself yesterday. Daniel wasn't used to being alone after sex, that was all. He hadn't ever thought about it, he just always stuck around afterwards, sleeping or talking or smoking. Frankly, the people he slept with usually wanted him to linger.

But he wasn't alone. Alex was maybe five yards away. If Daniel took two steps to the side, he could probably see Alex in bed. He was being a giant baby, that was all.

Little bubbles had appeared around the edges of the soup, so he turned off the gas and took out some plates and bowls. And the cheese looked melted, so he cut the sandwiches into triangles and slid them onto plates. While he was bringing everything over to the table, Alex came out of the bedroom. He was dressed, now, in pajama pants and a T-shirt, and he looked rumpled and sweet. Daniel tried not to stare. He was trying, he reminded himself firmly, to be cool—or, failing that, to at least act normal.

"Anything interesting happen at work?" Daniel asked, because that usually got Alex going—there was always a kid who insisted that his stuffed stegosaurus needed a vaccine or an asshole parent who thought Alex would threaten a kid with dire medical consequences for not going to bed on time. Daniel always liked hearing about that—loved glimpses into what Alex was like at work.

"Lots of teething babies," Alex said. "Lots of tired new parents."

"Did you ever want kids of your own?" Daniel asked, and then immediately wanted to die. *What the fuck, Daniel?*

Alex finished chewing his bite of grilled cheese. "No, not once I realized it wasn't happening for me," he said easily, and Daniel realized that people probably asked Alex this all the time. Probably every day, once they realized he was single. "What about you?"

"God no." Daniel tore the crust from half his sandwich into pieces and dropped them into his soup. "It was hard enough work being a kid." Sometimes Daniel still felt like he was mostly a kid himself, but this was probably not something he ought to admit to someone who had a graduate degree and washed his can opener.

"What if you married a woman, though?" Alex asked, swirling circles into his soup with his spoon.

What the fuck kind of question was that to ask someone you had just slept with? Okay, Daniel knew they weren't dating—they were friends having sex, that was what Daniel had offered and what Alex had implicitly agreed to. It wasn't fair for Daniel to play by rules Alex didn't know about.

"I'm not really planning on getting married, you know?"

Daniel said, because that was the only honest answer he could possibly give.

"You're young," Alex said, which was true but also irrelevant and kind of dismissive. But then he looked up and there was a smile on his face, tiny but real. "Thank you for dinner."

"Any time," Daniel mumbled.

Alex washed the dishes while Daniel tried to find something to watch on television. There was nothing even remotely interesting except a baseball game, so he turned it off.

"Want to read?" Daniel called into the kitchen. They did that sometimes, either on opposite ends of the sofa or with Daniel curled up sideways on the armchair and Alex sprawled on the sofa. Usually Alex read a medical journal and Daniel either read one of the books on gardening that he had taken out of the library or that book about elves and talking trees that Miriam was obsessed with and, amazingly, he had then found on Alex's bookshelf. He took the elf book from the shelf now and lay down on the sofa. At this rate, he'd be finished by 1980.

Alex didn't say anything, and the sink wasn't running so he knew Alex had heard him. And then a hot flush of embarrassment swept over him—maybe he was supposed to leave. It wasn't even nine, and Daniel didn't usually leave until close to ten, but maybe Alex didn't want him there.

"Or should I head home?" Daniel called into the kitchen, hoping he sounded casual, as if going home wasn't any better or worse for him than staying and watching television or reading.

This wasn't working. Their friendship depended on Alex being blunt and Daniel being straightforward. Alex was going to keep assuming that Daniel meant what he said and so he should say what he fucking meant.

But Alex got there first. He came out of the kitchen, drying his hands on the dish towel. "I don't want you to leave. I thought..." His gaze traveled down Daniel's bare chest.

"Or we could find other ways to occupy ourselves?" Daniel tossed the book on the coffee table and stretched his arms over his head. He didn't miss the way Alex tracked the movement.

"We could," Alex agreed, one of those rare playful smiles working at his mouth. He sat on the edge of the sofa near Daniel's head, and Daniel had to crane his neck to look upside down at him, but on the bright side this brought Alex's thigh right next to Daniel's face. "You," Alex said, "walking around my kitchen with your shirt off and your jeans half undone." He shook his head.

Daniel sort of didn't know what to do with that, with the knowledge that Alex wanted him that way. Which was absurd, because they had just had sex; obviously Alex was interested. "I kind of really want you to fuck me. If that's not your, um, cup of tea, then like I said, I'm easy to please. And we've never talked about whether you like doing that or—well—I could definitely fuck you, or we could get off in some other way." He was blathering, but he felt like all of that needed to be said. He smashed his mouth against the soft cotton covering Alex's thigh, mainly to shut himself up.

"Okay," Alex said.

"Okay?" Daniel wasn't sure which part of that garbled nonsense was okay, and didn't get a chance to ask because Alex was climbing over him on the couch, the weight of him a welcome pressure.

"I'd like to fuck you." The words made something go hot and tight in Daniel's belly. Alex *wanted* that, which made Daniel really, really want it. He had needed to hear what Alex wanted, *that* Alex wanted.

CHAPTER TEN

They kissed for a while, tangled up on the couch, a lot of the urgency from earlier gone, and also much of the tentativeness. Daniel didn't hesitate before sticking his hand down Alex's pants and grasping him, sticky hot and already hard. "Get these off," Alex said, tugging at Daniel's jeans, and Daniel felt another thud of desire at the request.

Daniel got to his feet and kicked his jeans off, then Alex tugged him back to the couch, astride his lap.

"Do you get fucked a lot?" Alex asked, sliding a hand down the small of Daniel's back. Daniel shuddered at the touch. He knew it was just a practical question, but Alex's voice was rough and low and Daniel wanted him to keep talking.

"Uh. No," Daniel admitted. It had only happened a few times at all. It had been a while since he'd slept with anyone other than Jacob and Lauren, and that wasn't what they were into. They probably would have worked something out if he had asked, but—

"But you like it?" Alex dipped his fingers into the crease of Daniel's ass, resting a fingertip right over his hole. Daniel let out a shaky breath, his forehead resting against Alex's shoulder. He'd have thought it was a tease if it was anyone other than Alex.

"Yeah, fuck, I do." He pushed back, hoping Alex got the idea. "And I like the idea of you doing it."

"I'll be careful," Alex said—just a plain statement of fact, delivered as simply as he would announce that he was going to answer the phone—and Daniel didn't think he'd ever needed the reassurance less.

* * *

Alex would never have called himself an inconsiderate lover—he made sure that the men he slept with got what they wanted and only what they wanted. He didn't use anyone, at least not any more than he was himself being used, and maybe having one-off sex in the bathroom of a gay bar was inherently using one another, he didn't know—but he wasn't used to thinking much about his sexual partners beyond what they did together.

This all sounded awful in his head and he should probably never say any of it aloud, especially to Daniel, who seemed to exclusively have sex with friends, and sometimes to actually make friends through having sex. One of the times they had gone to a club together, Daniel had gotten the number of the man he'd blown in the bathroom, and now that man sometimes brought mulch and seedlings to Daniel's garden. At the time, Alex had thought this was endearingly ridiculous in a typically Daniel way; now he was both jealous and confused.

With Daniel on his lap, and then—after convincing Daniel that he couldn't stay on the sofa if he wanted to get fucked—in his bed, Alex felt like he was in new territory. He really didn't like new territory, generally speaking, but new territory that involved Daniel sprawled out naked on his bed—that he could deal with. He hoped. He just didn't know how to do this. He could make it good for both of them, physically, but this was *Daniel*. He knew Daniel; worse, Daniel knew him. They knew one another kind of horrifyingly well and now they were going to fuck.

"Stuff's in the drawer," Alex said, and Daniel rolled over, exposing the long line of his back, the curve of his ass, as he reached for the nightstand.

"Wow," Daniel said. "A lot happening in here."

CHAPTER TEN

Alex propped himself up on an elbow and looked over Daniel's shoulder. There was a box of condoms, a jar of Vaseline, some lotion, a tube of KY Jelly, and a fairly basic dildo. He wondered which of these could possibly be unfamiliar to Daniel, and if it was either of the lubricants, Alex was faintly horrified as to what Daniel's previous experiences with being fucked had been like.

"The Vaseline is for anal sex," Alex said, in case Daniel didn't know this. "The KY Jelly is okay for anal sex, but it's better for jerking off. Also, you can't use Vaseline with condoms, so if you're using a condom, you're stuck with the KY."

He realized belatedly that he had just delivered a gay sex lecture to Daniel, which was probably condescending and awful. But Daniel just picked up the tube of KY and examined it thoughtfully. "I've only used condoms with women."

"I caught gonorrhea ten years ago and it was slightly traumatic," Alex said. "So if the person I'm with isn't sure, or if I've heard that something's going around, I make sure to use condoms." And then he wanted to die because talking about gonorrhea had to be the worst pillow talk anyone had ever attempted.

"Oh yeah. I caught that in college. Not a good week," Daniel said easily, squeezing a little lubricant onto his fingers. "Did you want to use a condom tonight?"

"I, um, I don't have anything. Did you want to?"

"No, me neither. And the only people I've been with lately are Lauren and Jacob, and we use condoms for—God, sorry, that's probably not a topic you want to hear about."

"Yes, discussing our experiences with venereal disease is much sexier."

Daniel laughed, even though Alex kind of hadn't been joking.

He didn't like to think about Daniel with anyone—although the fact that he had only been with those two friends of his lately was...interesting. He decided to think about that later, maybe, because now Daniel was stroking his own erection with his lubricant-covered fist. That had been good enough to watch earlier, when Alex had been coming down off his own orgasm, but now he could take a proper interest.

He replaced Daniel's hand with his own and gave his shaft the kind of firm pull Daniel seemed to like, moving his thumb roughly over the head as he had seen Daniel do. Daniel groaned and reached for him, pulling Alex half on top of him.

"You like that?" Alex asked, a little redundantly because it was obvious that Daniel did, based on the sound he just made, but it was what Alex would ask any partner. Sometimes he just needed to hear out loud that he wasn't getting things wrong.

"'S really good," Daniel said, thrusting into Alex's fist.

"Roll over." He wanted to ask if Daniel liked to be opened up a lot or only a little, but decided Daniel hadn't done this enough for anything other than the maximum amount of prep.

He slid a pillow under Daniel's hips and took a moment to just look at him, spread out on Alex's bed. The light was still on in the living room, so it was bright enough for Alex to see. Daniel looked good like this, hair a mess, his cheek resting on his tanned arms as he watched Alex. Alex moved down the bed between Daniel's legs and reached for the Vaseline. He scooped out just a little and rubbed it over Daniel's hole, then watched him shiver.

"Do you do this to yourself?" Alex asked. He probably ought to know; it probably mattered how new Daniel was to this. But really he just wanted to imagine Daniel touching himself.

"I can't get it to feel right," Daniel said. Which probably

meant that at least he knew what *right* was supposed to feel like. Good.

Alex eased the tip of a finger inside, not really doing much of anything, but Daniel buried his face in the pillow. "Good or bad?" Alex asked.

"Good," came Daniel's muffled reply.

He slid his finger deeper, slowly—he had to go slowly, because Daniel was just too tight. When Alex was new to this, the logistics had seemed impossible, and now they sort of did again. Watching his finger slide in and out, feeling the tight, hot clench of Daniel around him, he didn't know how he was going to fit himself inside.

Which was ridiculous, obviously, and a silly thing to waste time thinking about and yet—

"You're really tight," Alex heard himself say.

Daniel groaned and pushed back, as if he liked hearing Alex talk. Which—okay. Some people did. They were usually shit out of luck if they were with Alex, though.

"You feel good," Alex said, trying it on. And yes, there was another groan. He twisted his finger, searching until Daniel swore. "How does that feel?"

"Fuck off, how does it feel," Daniel muttered. "Good, and you know it. Now do it again."

Alex laughed, then did it again.

"I'm going to add another finger. Do you think you can take it?"

Daniel glared at him over his shoulder. "Are you teasing me?"

"I'm trying to."

Daniel rolled over onto his back, dislodging Alex's finger. "Want to watch you try to tease me."

When Alex slid two fingers in, Daniel did watch him, but not his hand—his face. Alex didn't know what to make of that, only that he couldn't possibly look back at Daniel, so instead he kissed the inside of Daniel's knee, watching his own fingers disappear inside Daniel's pink hole, the dark flush of Daniel's erection.

He added another finger and bent to take Daniel into his mouth, wanting to keep him hard.

"Don't," Daniel said, and so Alex didn't. "I'm too close. And—keep talking, okay?"

"Okay. Have you ever come like this? Just from being fingered?"

"Never tried." He sounded a little strained as Alex opened him up, but he was still hard.

"I can." Alex twisted his fingers and watched Daniel bite his lip. "But it's time-consuming."

Daniel's eyes were dark. "You say that like it's a bad thing. Alex. Do you ever do it this way?"

Alex knew what he meant—he was asking whether Alex liked to be fucked. But all Alex could think of was that he had never done anything this way, had never been, as Daniel was now, open and cheerful and chatty on someone else's bed. "Yeah," he said. "I liked to be fucked when I'm in the mood for it."

"Oh God, can I?"

"Right now?" Alex asked, incredulous. It wasn't the kind of question he was used to being asked when he had three fingers in someone's ass.

"No, don't you dare. Wait your turn."

Alex laughed again. He was used to talking during sex, to some extent—it was necessary, the most efficient manner of figuring out whether he was doing the right thing. But what they had been doing wasn't that kind of talking. This was a conversation, like any of the thousand other conversations they'd had, except they were fucking in the middle of it.

While they were talking, he had gotten Daniel about as ready as he was going to get. "How do you want to do this?" Alex asked. "Hands and knees?"

"Nah, I'm lazy. Just come here."

And so Alex did. He slicked himself and braced over Daniel on one arm, then lined himself up as best he could—this was objectively the worst position, he didn't know why he agreed to it—and then allowed himself a glimpse of the dark, dark blue of Daniel's eyes before pushing in.

There was no way this felt good for Daniel—he was still too tight and it had probably been too long—and that was the thought that kept Alex still, that kept his face buried in Daniel's neck and trying his best not to move.

"Come on," Daniel whispered. "Come on. Feels good."

It was on the tip of Alex's tongue to ask if he was sure, but then Daniel wrapped his legs around Alex's waist to get some leverage and Alex felt himself slide even deeper.

It was too easy. It shouldn't have been that easy. They weren't talking anymore, but it still felt like all the other time they had spent together, but with this, with the slick heat of their bodies, the tightening coil of pleasure. It felt like something it probably wasn't, like something more than Alex had bargained for, and which he wasn't going to get anyway.

When Daniel got a hand around himself, his mouth seemed to seek out Alex's, or maybe it was the other way around, but they were both too far gone to kiss. Alex remembered those kisses from the other night, kisses that had stretched out until they were asleep, sharing breath, sharing—

He didn't think he was going to be able to hold on any longer. "I'm going to—"

"Do it. God, do it. Inside me," Daniel added, answering the question Alex hadn't had the presence of mind to ask.

When he came, it was with the vague awareness that Daniel was coming too, that Daniel's grip on his shoulders had tightened to the point that he was going to bruise, that his stomach was wet with Daniel's release. He couldn't bring himself to move, as remnants of pleasure shook their way through him.

"You okay?" Daniel asked some time later.

"I'm supposed to be asking you that," Alex mumbled into Daniel's shoulder, breathing in the scent of his shampoo. He was still inside Daniel and on top of him, probably crushing him, and he ought to think about getting up and getting cleaned off. He did none of those things, and instead burrowed his face further into Daniel's neck.

"Do you always get like this after sex?"

That made Alex prop himself up just enough to look at Daniel's face. "Like what?"

"You're pretty blissed out." Daniel stroked a hand down Alex's back. "You were like this before, too."

"Not really," Alex answered honestly. The truth was that usually he got dressed—or, more typically, zipped himself up—and carried on with his evening. He didn't usually let himself go like this. Christ, he was *still* inside Daniel. Not that Daniel seemed to be complaining about it—but would Daniel complain about anything? Alex wasn't sure. He eased himself out.

"I'm going to take a shower." Except, no, Daniel really ought to get the first shower, he probably needed it. "Unless you want it? Or you could—it's a really small shower, but—"

"I've used your shower," Daniel said. "Just throw me a wet washcloth and then I'll take a shower after you."

Later, when they were both washed up, Daniel touched Alex's arm. "Do you want me to head home? Or I can stay. It's fine either way.

Alex needed the sleep, and he likely wouldn't get much with Daniel next to him.

"Stay," Alex said without thinking too hard about it.

Daniel looked pleased as he put on a spare pair of Alex's pajamas, and he looked pleased as he got into Alex's bed, and he looked pleased when they turned off the light, and so that was what Alex thought about instead.

Chapter Eleven

"Shit," Daniel said when they were getting dressed the next morning. It was their third attempt to put on clothes, the first two having gotten derailed with more sex, not that Daniel was complaining. "I hurt you." He pointed at Alex's hips, where purplish bruises stood out against his fair skin.

"There's some on my shoulders too," Alex said, turning around so Daniel could see. "I bruise easily."

"I'm really sorry. I didn't realize I was being that rough."

"You really weren't. And I don't mind." Alex's cheeks went a pretty shade of pink, and only then did Daniel understand—Alex *really* didn't mind. Well, then. Daniel didn't mind a bit of roughness either, didn't mind getting marked up, didn't mind much of anything, at least not anything he had run across yet. He had thought Alex would be fussier, though—which would have been fine, of course, but the knowledge that he wasn't sent a bolt of want through him.

He must have been looking dopey, because Alex came over and kissed him.

"You were right," Alex said.

"About what?"

CHAPTER ELEVEN

"You said it's nicer with friends. No wonder you sleep with all your friends if it's always like this."

Daniel felt his stomach drop. He *had* said that. He had pitched this whole idea to Alex as a normal thing for friends to do. He shouldn't be surprised that Alex thought this was just business as usual for him.

"You know you're not just any old friend, right?" Daniel asked. "You're not the mulch guy I trade handjobs with." Why was he talking about the mulch guy? Why, Daniel? "I mean, you know I..." He trailed off, not knowing how to finish that sentence. "You know I like you best?" he finally said, inanely, and as the words left his mouth he knew that the most honest thing he could have said was *I love you.*

It should have come as a surprise, but somehow it didn't.

"I know you like me best, Daniel," Alex said, but it sounded like he was humoring him.

It was too early, and Daniel wasn't awake enough to have a serious conversation, not that he had any idea what he could possibly say anyway. So he walked with Alex to the clinic even though it was out of his way and then went home.

His building was quiet. Blanca and Miriam would be at work. In the garden were a handful of kids too little for school. Their parents were gathered on a bench Daniel had found in a salvage yard a few weeks earlier. He made a mental note to find another one and maybe a small table. But there wasn't anyone around he could talk to. Lauren and Jacob would be at work too, and this didn't really feel like something he could talk to them about anyway, since the last time he had tried to talk to them about Alex it hadn't gone well.

The person he really ought to talk to was Mary, because she knew Alex better than anyone and would probably have an idea of what Daniel could say—or how he could say it, or even if he ought to say anything in the first place. But he wasn't sure if Alex would think that was going behind his back.

What he didn't want to do was spend the morning in his apartment, marinating in his own confusion. If he sat still, he was just going to feel all the places on his body where Alex had touched him last night, all the places Alex had been. Yesterday, he had pulled every weed and straightened every brick and rock in the garden, and there was nothing he could do to it right now without ruining something.

For one wild moment he considered calling his dad. His father, though, would decide that there was no problem at all, would somehow conclude that because Daniel had feelings for Alex, therefore Alex was in love with Daniel, and nothing Daniel could possibly say would make him think otherwise. His father was fundamentally incapable of envisioning a world where things didn't work out for his only child.

His mother wasn't like that at all—she was a dyed-in-the-wool cynic, but it wasn't like he could call her and talk about how he had convinced his best friend to fuck him and now was sad about it. That was not the kind of relationship they had, thank God. Also, she loved Alex and would probably be furious with Daniel for sullying his virtue or something. She would wind up scolding Daniel for making a mess of things.

Which, actually, might be exactly what he needed. Maybe he needed someone to tell him exactly how badly he'd screwed up and then he'd figure out a way to fix it.

He thought about getting on the subway to her apartment, but if she wasn't there, he'd be alone and annoyed on the Upper West Side and then he'd really be at loose ends. So he let himself into his apartment and dialed her number from memory. It rang for long enough that he was about to give up. She might not even be in town. He had given up trying to keep track of where she was.

But then she picked up. "Hello," she said, managing to pack those two syllables full of annoyance.

"Mom?"

"Daniel?" Now she sounded worried. "What's the matter?"

"Nothing, I just—"

"It's nine. In the morning."

He realized belatedly that not only was this early for him, but it was early for her, too. She had been keeping theater hours for over a decade and had never been much of a morning person to begin with. He had definitely woken her up. "Sorry, Mom, I forgot. I'll call back—"

"Like hell you will. What's the matter?"

"I, uh." He didn't know how to start. "Do you want to get lunch?" That would buy him a couple of hours to take a shower and think of what to say.

"Are you calling from the hospital?"

"What? No—"

"The police station?"

"Mom. I'm fine."

"We're both awake before ten. Nothing about this is fine, Daniel. Of course I'll buy you lunch, but I'm going to spend the next three hours thinking about every possible thing that could have gone wrong."

"It's not like that. I promise. I, well. It's about Alex."

"Is *he* in the hospital? The police station? No, he'd never get arrested, and if he were in either of those places, then you'd be right there with him. Does the clinic need money? No, he'd have called me himself."

"You give money to the clinic?" he asked, momentarily distracted.

"Don't be boring, Daniel," she said, which really wasn't an answer. "Let's see. If something were wrong with Alex's family, then you would just say so, instead of being tiresome. Oh, did one of you realize you were in love with the other? Which of you is correct and which of you is stupid?"

"Mom!"

"Lunch, eleven thirty, the usual place."

"Are they even open that early?"

She hung up.

Two hours later, he was walking into the Italian restaurant on the east side of Tompkins Square Park. According to the sign on the door, they opened at eleven, so at least his mother hadn't made the owner open just for her, which he absolutely wouldn't put past her. She was already there, sitting at her favorite table, in a dark corner of the restaurant that she said made her feel mysterious, like a man in a fedora was about to make a complete fool of himself over her.

"I ordered drinks," she said by way of greeting. Indeed, there was a pair of gin and tonics on the table.

He didn't point out that it wasn't even noon, just sat down and downed half his drink. "Thanks."

"Out with it." She tapped pink-varnished fingernails on the table.

"You know, you're too eager to hear about this. I'm your son."

"You're my boring son, is what you are. You're also an adult, and *you* called *me*, so you can get off your high horse. Is that Alex's shirt you're wearing?"

"How do you even—yes, yes it is. God." Daniel's shirt was

in no state to be worn, so Alex had given Daniel a plain gray T-shirt. Daniel hadn't hesitated to put it back on even after his shower. "Anyway. So." He told his mother everything, starting from that dinner with Paul and Mary, leaving out anything explicit.

"You love him," his mother said. At some point two plates of food that neither of them had ordered appeared in front of them. Daniel was eating his more distractedly than the food probably deserved.

"Well, he's my best friend." At his mother's unimpressed look, he sighed. "I—yes, what I'm feeling is more than that. Or different from that, at least."

"And you knew that before you offered to…" She waved her hand in a vague gesture, thank God, instead of attempting to finish that sentence with something like "have casual sex" which he didn't need to ever hear his mother say.

"Yeah. I think I did."

"So, you've deceived him, at least a little. You told him that you'd be doing things as friends. But you weren't." She paused, frowning. "Maybe deceit is the wrong word. It's the sort of secret that most people might understand, but I don't think Alex would."

"He never needs to find out," Daniel protested.

His mom looked at him in a way that made Daniel want to sink in his seat.

"He depends on people being honest with him. Completely honest, not just politely honest. You need to tell him what you actually want."

"I don't know what I actually want."

"Well, you need to figure that out, and then you need to tell him."

"Or, I could just not make my problems into his problems. None of this is his fault. I don't need to put all this on him."

"No, you don't need to," his mother said. "But you should. He should get a choice. You might think this is all in your head, that you're the only person affected, but you brought him into it. If he were an acquaintance or someone you could see yourself walking away from, it wouldn't matter. But if you keep this from him, you'll be deceiving him every step of the way from here on out."

"I don't want to make him uncomfortable or upset. He's going to feel guilty."

"You're the only one who's allowed to be feel bad?"

"What? No, of course not."

"It's your job to make sure everyone else is happy all the time? Look, I've seen how you accommodate Alex. You fit yourself into the spaces where he has room for you. He's very—I'm trying to come up with a kind way to say 'rigid.' You make sure he has everything he needs and when he needs it."

"I don't mind doing those things," Daniel said, feeling defensive.

"Daniel, my poor darling. I know you don't. I've spent half your life following Harry around and the other half arranging things so that your father's life was as perfect as it could be. I don't regret any of it. There's nothing wrong with taking care of the people you love."

He didn't know what to say to that. Obviously, he knew that his mother had done those things, but he never really thought of her as…well, she wasn't a pushover. She wasn't easygoing. Most of the time she wasn't even nice.

"But you can't lie about it," she went on. "You can't give people things they don't want or don't know about. Keeping this from Alex would be a lie by omission. And if there's a chance that he feels the same way that you do, it would be wrong of you to not give him a chance to tell you."

"But what if he doesn't?"

There was nothing his mother could say to that, obviously, and she didn't try.

* * *

Daniel was acting weird at dinner, cutting his chicken into tiny pieces and pushing them around his plate, but not eating any of them. His Coke sat untouched. His napkin was in shreds on the table. Alex was left attempting to carry the conversation, which made for a sorry state of affairs.

"I want to talk to you," Daniel finally said, and Alex was nearly relieved, even though there was no way anything Daniel had to say in this mood was going to be good news.

Last summer, Daniel had gone out of town to cover a music festival in some godforsaken field in Pennsylvania. And then this past winter, he spent three weeks traveling with a band for a profile he was writing for a magazine. Alex figured tonight's news was something like that.

"I think I misled you," Daniel said, looking up from his plate before quickly looking away. Failing to make eye contact was usually Alex's specialty, so this was a bit of a surprise, even more than the idea that Daniel had somehow misled him.

"I...okay," Alex said. "What about?"

"When I suggested that we sleep together as friends. I mean, obviously that's a thing people do, that's a thing I do, but I don't—that's not what I wanted to do with you."

Alex's eyes were wide. "You didn't want to sleep with me?"

"No—God—I mean of course I wanted to. I think I'm in love with you. No, scratch that, I'm definitely in love with you. A lot. And I think I've known for a while, but I didn't want to fuck things up. I should have told you instead of just trying to get you into bed, but that's what I did, and now I'm trying to make it right by telling you the truth."

Alex very nearly blurted out that actually Daniel had done exactly the right thing by not telling him any of that, that absolutely no good could possibly come of Alex knowing that Daniel loved him, and furthermore, was Daniel out of his mind? But Daniel was clearly distraught over this and Alex knew he couldn't say any of those things.

"I see," Alex said slowly. "What do you want me to do about this?"

Daniel sank down in his chair, as if he was trying to get under the table. "You don't have to do anything. I just thought I ought to tell you, so I wasn't sleeping with you under false pretenses."

Alex couldn't imagine how Daniel keeping that information to himself would have constituted false pretenses, but he had long since accepted that most people operated on a sense of justice or ethics that had nothing to do with reason.

Alex obviously had to say something. Daniel was crawling out of his skin and likely needed to go haul things around his garden for a while until he settled down, but for now he was stuck here with Alex.

"I don't think you did anything wrong," Alex said, because this seemed like the most important thing, and also the only fact he could drag out of the thicket of his thoughts and put into words. What remained in the thicket, unspoken and barely even acknowledged, was the fact that Alex was fairly certain he was in love with Daniel too. He had known this for a while, in the way that it was possible to know something while resolutely refusing to think about it. Now, though, Alex was going to have to think about it, and he wanted to be as far as possible from Daniel when that happened, otherwise he would do something stupid like actually admit it out loud.

Alex looked at the uneaten chicken on Daniel's plate, at the red Formica of the table, at anything and everything that wasn't Daniel's face.

"I want things to stay the way they are," Alex went on, pulling another fact out of the thicket. This was true, if not the whole truth. Alex could utter that sentence at almost any hour of the day, any day of the year, and it would be correct. People were forever deceiving themselves into accepting variety as a substitute for quality, for safety. When Alex found something that worked, he kept it that way.

What worked was Daniel being his friend—his best friend, the closest friend he'd ever had, someone he saw nearly every day and thought of before making any decision, but still: a friend. When he had thought that sex was going to be a part of that, Alex had been—well, pleased was an understatement, and now was really not the time to remember— No. He slammed the door on last night.

Last night didn't change anything. Alex was an adequate friend, but he'd be terrible at anything else. He'd always assumed that—dating, being in love, whatever you wanted to call it—was for other people, like noisy bars and organized religion and other things that most people seemed to like but which left him cold and a little upset.

There was no room in Alex's life for another person. He had always known that, and that understanding would have been enough to stop him from looking for any kind of lasting relationship even if he had known how to go about finding one. But when he thought back to this past Sunday, to how desperate he had been to—to get rid of Daniel, there was no other way to look at it—that fact was starkly clear. Daniel had wanted to cook him dinner and, probably, have sex with him, and Alex had all but shut the door in his face. And that had been after Daniel spent the entire weekend bending over backwards to please Alex—making sure he had the food he preferred, the music he enjoyed, and time to himself. Alex hadn't even noticed Daniel was doing it, hadn't noticed Daniel had been doing it since they met.

Daniel already twisted himself into pretzels to accommodate Alex. Imagine the chore it would be to bend himself any further. Alex didn't want their friendship to turn into a version of whatever personal martyrdom Daniel was performing when he visited his awful grandmother.

"Okay," Daniel said, and Alex didn't need to see his face to know that he was crushed.

"Why did you have to tell me all that?" Alex asked, suddenly annoyed that Daniel had brought this on both of them.

"Because I always tell you the truth."

Alex knew that was true—he *loved* that it was true—and he was annoyed with Daniel anyway, because things had been going fine, and now they weren't.

Daniel was looking at him, clearly waiting for him to say something else, but Alex couldn't think of anything. It had been several minutes since either of them had touched their food, the pretense of the meal long since dropped, and they must have been giving off an air of tension because no waiters had approached to clear the table.

"I need to go," Alex said, and got to his feet. He took fifteen dollars out of his wallet and dropped it on the table, more than enough to cover both their meals. Then he turned on his heel and started to leave.

"Alex," he heard. He turned around. Daniel was standing up, holding out Alex's jacket. "You forgot this."

"Thanks," Alex managed.

"Also, you don't need to leave."

"I do."

"Then I'm leaving too." Daniel took out his wallet and threw an apparently random assortment of bills on the table. At least they were tipping the waitstaff exorbitantly for forcing them to participate in what was undoubtedly a scene.

Alex made for the door. "I need to be alone."

"No," said Daniel, coming up beside him.

"No?" It was so rare to hear the word from Daniel's mouth that Alex was momentarily startled.

"I don't think we're done talking," Daniel said, calm but insistent.

"*I'm* done!" Alex opened the door, then held it open for Daniel, who mumbled "Thanks," because apparently they were both incapable of fighting like normal people.

"I don't need to actually talk or anything," Daniel said, sounding fully dejected. "I just don't want you to leave me when you're upset with me. I really hate it, actually. I should have told you a long time ago, but...I don't know."

"You like to suffer to make other people happy," Alex suggested.

"No! I usually like doing what makes you happy. I like making the people I—care about happy."

Alex would have bet that Daniel had nearly said love, and before now Alex didn't think he would have even noticed, because it was obvious every minute of the day that Daniel loved him. He decided to think about that later, or perhaps never. He turned his attention to the sidewalk, littered with cigarette butts and ancient wads of chewing gum.

"Like you give up entire weekends to drive to Massachusetts to be abused by your grandmother," Alex said.

"Oh, for fuck's sake. Do you think—did you just compare yourself to my grandmother?"

Alex thought it was obvious that he had, so he didn't bother answering. "I don't want to be a good deed that you make yourself perform."

"I—wow. Okay. So, I don't love my grandmother, or even like her, or harbor any warm feelings toward her whatsoever. I visit her to make sure she's being taken care of, and I could do that without ever listening to a word she says except that it really pisses her off to have to see me. For half an hour every few months she has to deal with the fact that I, her least favorite grandchild, am the only one who comes to see her. She hates every minute of it. I don't like it either, but it's totally worth it. I'd go twice as often if she lived closer."

Alex was at a loss for words. "That's...extremely petty."

"I know."

"Sometimes you take after your mother," Alex said.

"Thank you. Anyway, I'm sorry, I know you want to be alone and I'm being a pain in the ass. I know you need space and I'll always give it to you, but sometimes I need a few minutes of reassurance. I really just meant that I didn't want you to leave me until I knew that things between us were okay, and I know that now, so thank you."

It was true that Alex wanted to be alone, but he often wanted to be alone. Usually it was because he was just done coming up with words or arranging his face appropriately, but maybe that didn't need to be a problem with Daniel, who had seen him in that state often enough. Sometimes it was because things were too loud and he needed the quiet, controlled environment of his own apartment. But sometimes it was because he was afraid he was about to have an emotional response that was so disproportionate to the situation that it would alienate everyone around him. That, partly, was what he was worried about now.

But Daniel was wiping tears away from his eyes with a shaky hand, so disproportionate emotional responses were perhaps acceptable this evening. And if Daniel didn't want to be alone, if it made him sad to be left alone, Alex didn't want to let that happen.

"I want to give you what you want," Alex said. "I always want to do that. But I don't always know what that is." He thought that would have made Daniel feel better, but instead now there were more tears than he could wipe away with his fingers. He started using the hem of his T-shirt, which meant he was exposing himself in the middle of the sidewalk. Probably the reason Alex reached over and wiped away Daniel's tears with his own dry fingers was just to prevent public indecency.

"Let's find somewhere to sit," Alex suggested. At least they were in a place where two men having what was pretty obviously a lovers' spat in public wouldn't be remarkable. There might not be many places in the world where they could get away with this, but Manhattan below 14th Street was one of them.

He decided not to think about how the phrase *lovers' spat* seemed unobjectionable. This was not a normal sort of quarrel for friends to have. Even Alex knew that. They were near

St. Mark's church, which had a bench they could sit on and continue to have a public scene, so Alex led them in that direction.

"Sorry. This is stupid," Daniel said when Alex finally saw reason and produced a tissue for him to blow his nose.

"Nothing you do is stupid."

"That's a lie."

It was, sort of. Except—no. "You do a lot of unreasonable things," Alex said. "You stay up too late. You forget to eat. Sometimes you smoke cigarettes and you think I don't know but I can smell the tobacco on you. You don't take good enough care of yourself and it makes me feel crazy, because you are—" He tripped over the next words, because *you are precious to me* was a deranged thing to say and *the idea of you hurting yourself makes me want to throw you off a bridge* wasn't much better. "Because you matter the most. You're the most important thing in my life," he said, which was worse than either of his other options, but he said it anyway. "None of that's stupid, though."

Daniel was staring at him, which was exactly what anyone would do if they saw someone lose their grip on normal behavior, so Alex couldn't blame him.

They had reached the bench in front of the church. Daniel sat in a way that his body sort of tilted towards Alex's. If they were on Alex's sofa, he'd know that Daniel was about to do the thing where all his molecules just sort of spilled in Alex's direction until they were—for lack of a better word—cuddling. But Alex wasn't going to do that in public, even if they were below 14th Street, so he reached for Daniel's hand.

Handholding, public or otherwise, could be added to the list of things friends probably didn't do, along with publicly fighting and crying. "I'm holding your hand platonically," Alex announced, because even if his mind was in turmoil, he didn't want to give Daniel the wrong idea. The fact remained that he wasn't equal to any kind of romantic relationship and he didn't want to imply otherwise.

"Is this like how we had sex platonically?" Daniel asked, and then started to laugh. Alex might have thought that Daniel was laughing at him except for how Daniel squeezed his hand so hard Alex couldn't have let go if he tried.

Chapter Twelve

That could definitely have gone worse, Daniel told himself. It could have gone better, too.

He went home and called Lauren and Jacob to ask if they wanted to go see a band he was thinking of writing a piece about. He didn't want to be alone, but he also needed to see them to call off their arrangement. He had always figured it would be them who ended it, but last night he had sex with someone he loved, and he didn't think he could now enjoy sex with two people who loved one another. Envying the relationship of the couple you're fucking was probably just weird and against the rules.

When he got to the club, he spoke with the manager, who he knew, and the band's frontman, who he didn't, then settled in at a table off to the side where he wouldn't be disturbed. He must have looked as sorry as he felt, because the bartender sent over a drink he hadn't ordered. Or maybe the manager just wanted good publicity. Daniel pushed it aside for Lauren or Jacob to have. His sense of calm was too precarious right now to mess it up with alcohol.

They showed up twenty minutes later, took one look at him, and exchanged a speaking glance with one another. Daniel told them the whole miserable story while they waited for the band to start.

"I think he's been in love with you from the beginning," Jacob said. "It sounds like he's just freaking out."

"Give it time," Lauren agreed.

"You'll work it out."

Daniel raised his eyebrows. "You two want me to get together with Alex? I thought you didn't like him."

They looked at one another. "We don't dislike him. It's been pretty obvious that he's jealous of us, but he's also jealous *at* us, you know?" Jacob said.

On some level, Daniel knew this had to be true. Alex was perfectly cordial to Blanca and Miriam and all Daniel's other friends. Jealousy was the best explanation for that discrepancy.

"He's not exactly trying to charm us," Lauren said.

"He doesn't try to charm anyone," Daniel said. "I don't think he's ever tried to charm anyone in his life. He isn't charming in the least."

"Why do you look so happy about that?" Lauren asked.

Then the conversation turned to something else, and Daniel realized he already felt better.

That had to be something, that you could have your heart broken, at least a little, and be okay. And he was okay, or he would be.

It occurred to Daniel that despite talking for over half an hour and emoting all over the East Village, he had never asked Alex what he meant by wanting to keep things the way they were. Did Alex mean that he wanted to go back to how things were before they had sex? Or did he want to keep having sex and cuddling on the sofa and spending almost all their free time together? Because if it was the latter, Daniel didn't see how that differed from his ideal outcome. He didn't see how that differed from just being in love, because he didn't doubt that Alex loved him as much as he loved anyone, even if he never said so.

It also occurred to him that he really didn't want much to change either, and that he maybe should have mentioned this to Alex before dropping bombshells on him.

The band started their set, so Daniel took out his notebook and turned his attention to the music.

* * *

Alex walked back to his apartment, taking a long, slow, meandering route that was utterly inefficient but that let him make the most of a warm evening, even if it was slightly ruined by the smell of garbage and exhaust smoke, not to mention his unspeakable mood.

He didn't want to go home. He didn't want to be alone in an apartment where twenty-four hours earlier he had been with Daniel. It was stupid—Daniel had been there countless times before last night, and the fact that they'd slept together didn't change that.

That idea lodged in his mind: the fact that they had slept together maybe changed less than he thought. The fact that Daniel loved him maybe changed less than he thought, too. What mattered, maybe, was that Daniel had told him. He had said that he told Alex because he wanted to be honest, but that wasn't why people said they loved one another, or at least it wasn't the only reason. People said it because they wanted to hear it back.

And Alex hadn't done that, because that would have been

opening a can of worms that Daniel didn't deserve to have inflicted on him.

Except Daniel kind of already was dealing with that can of worms, and had been doing so willingly and enthusiastically for the past year and a half. And Alex had loved letting him. Alex loved the way Daniel slotted himself into Alex's life, loved making him smile, loved—loved Daniel, when it came right down to it.

Alex had fallen in love piecemeal, inch by inch, by slow degree. As if maybe by not thinking about it while it was happening, not acknowledging it, even in the privacy of his own mind, he could make it any less true. He fell in love with things that were painfully trite, like the overwhelming blue of Daniel's eyes, although nothing about them seemed trite when he was looking at them. And he fell in love with things that were just painful, like the easy friendliness with which Daniel treated his lovers and ex-lovers, none of whom ever seemed to go away. Well, Alex wasn't going to go away either, so he could hardly blame them.

He turned around before he got home and headed back across town. He reached Daniel's building in what was probably record time and buzzed Daniel's apartment. There was no answer, so he tried again.

"He went out," said the dark-haired woman who lived in the unit below Daniel's. Miriam, Alex remembered. She was sitting in the garden in the empty lot next door. "Some band he wanted to see."

Right. Daniel wouldn't have wanted to be alone after—after.

"Did he seem all right when you saw him?" Alex asked, which was probably nosy of him, and maybe rude, but he needed to know.

"Why don't you sit down, Alex," she said, patting the bench beside her. "It's pretty, isn't it?" She gestured at the garden.

And it was—he already knew that, had watched it spring up from a legitimately frightening tetanus-filled disaster zone to something beautiful. Daniel had spent over a year carving this space out, his work not only unpaid but possibly ephemeral, as there was nothing stopping the city from tearing it all up. There was something dangerously naive about putting your heart into something that could be swept away on a whim. Except—was there really anyplace or anything safe and permanent enough for Daniel's heart? Alex didn't think so.

The problem might be the metaphor, as it so often was. The heart was meant as a stand-in for love, effort, devotion. In reality, the heart just plugged away until something stopped it. Maybe the metaphor wasn't that bad after all, because in Alex's experience, just plugging away was sometimes the hardest thing a person could do, the strongest proof of love and devotion a person was capable of. You dig a hole, you come to a new country, you learn a new language, you try your best, and then you do it again. You tell yourself that the risk of getting hurt is less than the risk of not trying at all.

Everett was right when he'd said that Daniel wasn't tough; Daniel was open and honest in a way that left him vulnerable to too many things. But he was sure and solid; he was resilient for the people he cared about and brave for the causes he thought were worth it. The night they met, Daniel had punched an enormous stranger, which at the time Alex had considered self-destructively idealistic but later understood as—yes—both self-destructive and idealistic, but also the impulse of a good person who wanted to step in front of any injustice he could.

The word Alex was looking for was *strong*—Daniel was strong.

He would weather a storm on a friend's behalf, and maybe even would welcome the opportunity to do so.

Alex didn't know what he had to offer, but he knew that he could trust Daniel to make it enough for both of them. He had so far, after all.

The sun was setting, which meant Alex had been sitting there for a while. He probably ought to say something to this nice lady who told him where Daniel was. In all likelihood she was stoned and had the forgiving understanding of time that all stoned people did, though, so Alex kept his mouth shut.

"Oh," Miriam said. "Look. Fireflies."

"What?" Alex knew the word, but thought he must have misunderstood.

"Lightning bugs."

And sure enough, there were a few flickering specks of light over by a flowering bush. Alex had lived in this city for over fifteen years and never seen one of these insects here. Had never seen them anywhere, for that matter. They belonged in the picture books he read to his nephew, in cartoons, not empty lots. It was as bizarre as seeing a unicorn, and Daniel had made it happen with a year of digging and planting and carefully tending something that otherwise wouldn't exist.

"Do you know where he went?" Alex asked Miriam.

She told him, and he suppressed a groan. Well, at least it wasn't in one of the outer boroughs, and there were worse fates than having to go north of Union Square.

Of course there were no goddamn cabs, because there never were in this neighborhood, and by the time he saw an empty cab he was five blocks from the nightclub, so he just walked the rest of the way.

A large man stationed at the door let him into the club, and all he had to do was find Daniel in a room that was filled with various kinds of smoke, almost vibrating with loud music, and crowded with bodies. If Alex led a horrible life, his eternal punishment would look something like this.

Daniel had once mentioned that he always sat on the side of the room, presumably so he wouldn't be disturbed by the cocaine-fueled orgies or whatever it was that was going on here. So Alex made his way around the perimeter of the room, skirting the bar and, after some rough going attempting to get past a throng of people, he spotted Daniel.

He was wearing a black T-shirt and a black leather jacket and, Alex presumed, black jeans. This was Daniel's equivalent of formal wear. Basically a tuxedo. His hair was loose and shiny in the dim light.

Daniel always looked good. Here, though, he looked good in the proper context; sometimes Alex forgot that Daniel's clothes weren't just random frayed garments, but an actual style. He was alternately writing in a notebook and glancing at the stage, and Alex belatedly realized that he was interrupting Daniel at work—something Daniel had never done to him in the entire time they had known one another. Well, it was too late for second thoughts.

With Daniel were Lauren and Jacob, but they didn't have their hands all over him for once, probably because he was working. They were sitting awfully close, but Alex supposed they'd have to be in order to hear one another, and besides, he reminded himself, that was none of his business.

When he reached the table (in order to reach it, he had to step over what seemed to be a pair of pants, which he added to the "none of his business" column), he was momentarily at a loss for what to do. It was too loud to just say Daniel's name. In order to tap his shoulder, he'd have to reach across Lauren. So he just stood there like an idiot, watching Daniel scribble on his notepad, until Lauren saw him.

She looked up and said, "Oh." At least that's what it looked like; it was far too loud to hear. She nudged Daniel, who looked up and immediately got to his feet. He climbed past Lauren and stood in front of Alex.

"What are you doing here?" Daniel asked.

Probably the sane and polite thing would be to say something like *gosh, Daniel, I'm sorry to barge in on your work-slash-threesome but I wanted to talk.* But it was too loud for formalities. "We're already together," Alex half shouted. "We're already together in every way, and if there's some other way you can think of, if there's something else you need, we can do that too."

He barely got out the last few words before Daniel's arms were around his neck, his face in Alex's hair.

* * *

Daniel didn't know which surprised him more: that Alex showed up at a nightclub to see him or that he stayed, calmly sipping a lukewarm mixed drink, acting almost friendly to both Lauren and Jacob.

"I only need to stick around until the end of this set," Daniel had said. "It'll be fifteen minutes, maybe? If you want to wait outside, I'll find you when I'm done. Or I can just meet you at your apartment."

But Alex had stayed, and he might be the only person in the history of Max's Kansas City to show up wearing a sweater vest. Daniel wished he had a camera.

When the set was over, Daniel kissed Lauren on the cheek, then she leaned over and kissed Alex's cheek too.

Outside, Alex visibly deflated with relief.

"That bad?" Daniel asked.

"I'm really happy you have friends to go to these things with," Alex answered, which Daniel thought was a sweet way of saying that he was never doing that again.

"Me too. Walk or cab home?"

"Walk. It's only fifteen minutes, unless you want—"

"If I cared either way, I wouldn't have asked," Daniel said. "You aren't going to get weird and start making me have preferences about everything now that we're—whatever we are. Which, um. We should talk about?"

He really didn't want to talk about it. He had talked enough about his feelings today to last a lifetime. His throat literally hurt from all the talking he had done and he kind of just wanted to go to bed. But he also knew that if he was wrong about what Alex had meant by showing up and saying what he said, Daniel would be devastated later on. Better to figure out now whether they were on the same page.

"For me..." Alex started, and then trailed off. Daniel didn't need to turn his head to know he was scowling. "I meant what I said about wanting to keep things the way they are. I want to keep seeing you every day and keep thinking about you all the time. I want you to keep falling asleep on me on the couch. I want—I want to keep loving you, all right? Because I have for a while." He said this as if he expected an argument. Daniel started to laugh. "Oh, for fuck's sake," Alex grumbled.

"No, no, keep going. This is romantic."

"No, it isn't. And it won't be. I don't have it in me. I think I'm going to be a terrible boyfriend, but I also think

I've been a terrible boyfriend for a while now. You're the only person—you're it for me. You've *been* it for me. So, that's what I want."

Daniel felt like the breath was knocked out of him. Like he had been hit in the gut but with—happiness or something. "Okay," he said. It was probably good that they were in public so he wasn't tempted to mortify Alex with a public display of affection. "Me too. To all of that. But you aren't terrible at any of this."

Alex made a skeptical sound. "As for the rest of it—the rest of whatever people do when they're..." He made a gesture between the two of them. "The rest of it is less important. If you want to sleep with other people, go for it. I won't like it, but I also don't like that you refuse to eat breakfast. I'll live."

"I already called it off with Lauren and Jacob. I don't like the idea of you with anyone else, and fair's fair. I mean—it's negotiable, but—"

"Wasn't planning on being with anyone else. I meant it when I said that it was nicer with you—better with you."

That hadn't been exactly what Alex had said, but Daniel was too happy to nitpick.

"I'll need time to myself, still," Alex went on.

"Yeah, me too," Daniel agreed, bumping Alex's shoulder with his own.

"I feel so shitty when I tell you to go away."

Daniel frowned. "That's not—that doesn't bother me in the least. When you need to be alone, I just go and do other things. And I need to be alone sometimes too. Like I said, I prefer knowing we're okay first, but that's not really what we're talking about."

"And you'll tell me if that stops being true." Alex sounded

nervous, and Daniel remembered the early days of their friendship, when Alex had seemed faintly surprised whenever Daniel turned up, as if he didn't understand that anyone might want to spend time with him. Daniel had dealt with that by continuing to show up until, finally, Alex had stopped looking so surprised. They were going to need to do that again, Daniel guessed. He'd wear Alex down with a campaign of reassurance.

"I promise," Daniel said. "What about tonight? Do you want me to go back to my apartment?"

"Absolutely not."

Alex had him against the wall as soon as the apartment door clicked shut behind him. It turned out there were a lot of walls on the way from the front door to the bedroom and Daniel got kissed against all of them.

It had been a long day, but some of Daniel's weariness dropped away at the first brush of Alex's lips against the sensitive place beneath Daniel's ear. Only some of it, though. He was still torn between sleep and arousal. Maybe Alex could tell how tired he was, because when they got to the bed, he undressed Daniel, not seeming to expect much in the way of participation.

"Anything you want? Or, I guess, anything you don't want?" Alex asked, his head already halfway to Daniel's lap.

Daniel shook his head. "I'll stop you if there's anything I don't like."

There was no teasing, just an extremely straightforward blowjob that was so *Alex* that Daniel almost laughed. When Alex pulled off and looked up, Daniel bit back a protest.

"Can you keep talking?" Alex asked. "Last night, I liked when you talked."

Daniel tried to remember if he had executed any especially

memorable dirty talk, but they had mainly just...talked. And Daniel had liked that too, had liked the constant reminder that this was Alex he was with.

"You're so pretty," Daniel said, petting Alex's hair and pushing it back a little to get a better look at him. "You're so—I could look at you all day." Alex shot him a look that was probably meant to be a glare, but it wasn't like he could talk back at the moment. "Right now a bouncer at that club is explaining to his boss that he let in a man dressed like an accountant, but he had to because this was the most beautiful man alive, what was he supposed to do. No, just deal with the compliment, Alex. I have a backlog of things to say about your pretty face."

Alex adopted a strategy of distracting Daniel by doing something very interesting with his tongue, but Daniel was undeterred.

"Your mouth," Daniel groaned. "I love when you purse your lips like you're irritated at everything in the world—everything that isn't me." He thumbed the corner of Alex's mouth, stretched around him, and felt Alex's answering moan everywhere in his body.

Alex pressed a hand firmly into Daniel's chest, shoving him down to the mattress. Daniel had a notion of where this was going and he liked it.

"If your goal is to shut me up, that won't work," Daniel said, reaching blindly for the nightstand drawer where Alex kept the Vaseline and tossing it down the bed to him.

"It's not," Alex said, and bit him on the inside of the thigh. "Just need to get inside you."

Daniel heard himself make a desperate, mortifying sound as he bent his knees, then felt slick fingers against his hole. Last night Alex had been so slow, so careful, but tonight there was none of that, only the same urgency that Daniel felt. Alex's fingers were rough, almost clumsy inside Daniel, his mouth hot on Daniel's cock.

"Your eyes," Daniel said, not wanting to give up his compliment attack quite yet. "So fucking pretty. I try to sneak looks when you aren't paying attention. They're this perfect shade of gray-blue and whenever I see anything like it—a sweater, a car, some weird fucking candy, I don't know—I think of you." Daniel probably could have done better than comparing Alex's eyes to weird candy—they're like ice, Daniel, you jackass—but his brain wasn't at its sharpest, and anyway he liked candy and sweaters a lot more than he liked ice.

Alex's fingers were gone and Daniel found himself being tugged by the hips and roughly flipped over, his knees nudged apart, Alex's teeth on his shoulder. "Need you," Alex muttered.

Daniel felt the way he had on the street, sucker-punched by joy, almost overwhelmed by it, his face hot with it. "I need you too," he said. "Please."

Alex pulled back for an instant and then was pushing in, thick and hot, and Daniel buried his face in the crook of his elbow because there was probably a limit to the number of times a person could say *please* before it got boring to listen to. He wasn't even sure what he was asking for, only that he'd get it.

It had been good last night, really good, and this was—he was tired and there was no way this was Daniel's best effort. But the thick slide of Alex into him, the heat of his breath on the back of Daniel's neck, the sounds he was making—it all added up to something almost painfully sweet, and then to something even more when paired with the hell of the day, the relief of that conversation, the promise of what lay ahead.

Alex was a heavy weight, his body around him and inside him and pressing him to the mattress. Daniel almost protested when Alex shifted to his knees, but then realized what Alex must be doing—watching himself, watching where they were joined. He bit the skin of his own wrist.

"Your ass," Alex said, something almost reverent in his wrecked voice. "Jesus. It's—I mean it looks good in jeans, but it looks better like this."

And probably Daniel shouldn't have needed any additional evidence that Alex was attracted to him, given what they were doing at that moment, but the knowledge shot through him anyway.

"I compliment your pretty eyes and you say things about my ass?" Daniel said, letting out a breathless laugh.

"Are you complaining right now?" Alex punctuated that with a particularly hard thrust at just the right angle that had Daniel swearing into the pillow.

Alex got a hand under him, around him, no finesse happening at all, just a few rough strokes and Daniel was gone, barely aware of Alex stiffening over him, coming inside him. Alex didn't pull out, didn't try to move away, and Daniel dimly thought that he could fall asleep like this, Alex still inside him.

And maybe he did fall asleep, because he was a bit startled when Alex pulled out, barely registered when Alex murmured a *shh* and turned off the hall light, returning a moment later with a warm washcloth. It probably ought to be embarrassing, being looked after like this, but it was kind of nice, and Daniel wasn't capable of moving anyway.

"Roll over," Alex murmured, nudging Daniel's shoulder. Either Daniel had summoned up enough strength to roll, or Alex did it for him, because the next thing he knew he was on a clean sheet, the ruined bedspread tossed aside, a clean coverlet spread over them both, and then nothing but sleep.

Chapter Thirteen

Perhaps if Alex lined up a row of pillows along the length of the bed, he could keep Daniel from tangling himself up in Alex's limbs. However, the fault was at least fifty percent Alex's, because there was no denying that Daniel was on his own side of the bed and Alex was not; there was also no denying that Daniel was facing the outside of the bed while Alex was facing Daniel. Alex, in fact, had an arm tight around Daniel's chest, his nose plastered against the back of Daniel's neck, Daniel's hair all over his face.

Upon reflection, Alex had to bump that up to an eighty percent likelihood this was his own doing. Ninety-five, even. Daniel was an innocent man.

He remembered what Daniel had said that first time they had woken up entangled—that first, mortifying morning that Alex couldn't regret, because it had set everything else in motion. He had casually offered to take care of Alex, like Alex's hard-on was a sink full of dishes.

Alex thought he understood a little better now, understood that Daniel wanted to make him happy and comfortable and satisfied, that doing so made Daniel happy too. That this was why they worked as friends, worked as whatever they were now.

It was past seven, though, and Alex needed to get ready for work. Instead, he nudged his nose against the nape of Daniel's neck.

Daniel must not have been too deeply asleep, because he hummed out a pleased sound. And then, maybe realizing where he was, wriggled a little closer.

"Morning," Alex murmured.

"Time is it?"

"Just past seven. You can go back to sleep, just lock the door when you leave."

"Stay a bit," Daniel mumbled, pushing his ass back against Alex's half-hard dick, just like he had that time a few weeks earlier. "Let me—"

"Yeah," Alex breathed. "Okay." He had put on pajama pants and a T-shirt before going to bed, but Daniel was still naked, and that thin layer of cotton made the entire situation more obscene, somehow, like Daniel was naked in bed *for* him. It wasn't true—Daniel was naked because he had passed out about ninety seconds after coming, had been soft and tired and pliant on Alex's bed, and just the sight of him had nearly been enough to get Alex hard again. The memory did the job now, and he thrust against the lush curve of Daniel's ass.

He thumbed Daniel's nipple with the hand that was already on his chest, kissed the spot below his ear that made him squirm, firmly ignored the fact that neither of them had brushed their teeth. He felt like he was doing something new, like this was some exotic sex act he had just discovered rather than just rubbing off on someone's admittedly perfect ass.

When Alex pulled down the waistband of his pants, Daniel lazily tossed him the tube of KY, and Alex made a note that half asleep and with his eyes shut, Daniel was capable of finding the lubricant. His cock found the crease of Daniel's ass and they both made a satisfied sound. Daniel shifted on the bed, the movement of his forearm giving away what he was doing beneath the sheet. Alex kicked off the sheet and pushed up on an elbow so he could watch. The angle changed, and now his erection was between Daniel's thighs, tight and hot, and he remembered last night, remembered the night before that, the welcoming yielding clench of Daniel's body, and maybe Daniel was remembering it too because his hand was moving faster now.

"You can—anything you want," Daniel said, pushing back in case Alex hadn't gotten his meaning. Alex bit back the urge to double-check, instead shifting so the sensitive, wet head of his erection rubbed against Daniel's hole. And, fuck, he was still a bit loose. Alex could probably slip inside, easy as that.

Alex decided to trust that Daniel meant it. He pressed, just a nudge, and the fluttering clench he felt in response sent him over the edge. He pulled back to watch himself come all over Daniel's ass, resisted the urge to apologize, then flipped Daniel over and swallowed his dick down.

"Holy shit," Daniel said afterwards, then stretched out with an extravagant yawn. He looked like he could fall back asleep, and the thought of that—Daniel, filthy, sleeping in Alex's bed while Alex was at work—was so unexpectedly and weirdly appealing that he didn't know what to do with it. But probably staring at a half-asleep Daniel wasn't the answer, so instead he took a shower.

He was only a little surprised when Daniel joined him, and not surprised at all when Daniel's agenda seemed to involve more kisses than actual cleaning up. So Alex washed them both while

Daniel tried to sneak kisses in, lazy kisses that weren't going to go anywhere and which Alex would probably remember all day.

* * *

On Thursdays, Daniel picked up lunch at a storefront that sold soup and pierogis. There was no English menu, just a handwritten list in Ukrainian pinned to the wall. But the owners knew by now that Daniel was picking up an order for Alex, who had once come over on a Sunday night to treat their granddaughter's strep throat, and so they knew what to give him and always threw extra fried cabbage pierogi into the bag for Mary and Daniel to fight over.

He waved to the receptionist and let himself into Mary's office, then set the food up on her desk. When Mary came in a few minutes later, she stood there with her hand on her hip and stared at him.

"Turn to the left," she ordered, collapsing into her desk chair. He did as he was told. "Tell me that's from Alex," she said, gesturing at the side of his jaw where he knew he had a bite mark. "Because for two days in a row he's had beard burn on his neck and he's been walking around *smiling*, and either it's you or he has a brain tumor, so give a girl some good news, all right? Tell me you idiots figured it out?"

"We idiots figured it out," Daniel confirmed, not seeing any reason to keep her in suspense. "Why didn't you just ask him?"

She leveled an unimpressed look at him as she bit a pierogi. "I did, and he turned so red the patients were going to think he had measles, so I took pity."

"You've never taken pity on anyone in your life," he said.

"Well, he ran away and I thought it would be unprofessional to chase him into an exam room. Same difference."

Alex came in then and sat in the chair beside Daniel.

"You should probably expect my mom to call you," Daniel warned him. "I kind of poured my heart out to her yesterday and she's embarrassingly overinvested in all this."

"Saturday is our shopping day," Alex said. "That's when we talk about you." He slid some fried onions onto his plate. "What?" he asked, apparently realizing Daniel and Mary were staring at him.

"I really feel like it wasn't Paul's fault that he thought you two were together," Mary said. "I think it's your fault that you didn't know you were together. This is my verdict." She pounded her stapler on her desk like a gavel.

"Fair," Daniel said. "Very fair."

"Eat that pierogi," Alex said. "You didn't have any breakfast."

It occurred to Daniel that he had possibly signed up for a lifetime of being told to eat things, a lifetime of making sure boring British soft rock was on the turntable, and if he didn't figure out some way to wipe this smug smile off his face, he wasn't going to be able to eat the pierogi.

Daniel managed to eat the pierogi anyway.

II

Part Two

August 1973

Chapter Fourteen

There were storms over the Midwest, apparently, so Daniel's flight didn't land until past midnight, and then there had been the usual ordeal of getting a cab at LaGuardia, so he hadn't gotten back to his apartment until nearly two in the morning.

Two wasn't even that late, especially since he was still on California time, and he often came home a lot later than that even in New York. But a day on a plane after a week working in San Francisco, and that hot on the heels of a music festival in upstate New York, and Daniel wasn't tired so much as just *done*. He wasn't leaving the five boroughs for the next month for any reason, and the sooner he could stop moving and collapse somewhere soft and clean, the better.

He lugged his suitcase up the stairs and the first thing he saw was a piece of lined notebook paper taped to his door. That was never a good sign. Usually it meant someone upstairs had a flood or there was a building-wide pest problem.

With a sense of foreboding, he tore the note down and unfolded it. Then his heart gave an extra little thump because that was Alex's handwriting, even and precise, the ballpoint pen pressed so hard against the paper that you could feel the shape of the letters underneath. "Daniel, I'm inside. I didn't want you to think you had an intruder. Alex." Daniel had the door unlocked in record time.

The apartment was dark, and Daniel set his suitcase down as quietly as possible before peering into the bedroom. Sure enough, Alex was in his bed, and yes, Daniel would have had the shit scared out of him if it hadn't been for the note.

"Hey," he whispered, just to see if Alex was anywhere near awake, but Alex didn't stir.

Alex hated Daniel's apartment, so maybe something awful had happened to Alex's apartment and he had needed somewhere to stay. But in that case, he'd probably get a room at a hotel. More likely, he just wanted to see Daniel as soon as possible and was willing to sleep in a strange bed in order to do so. Daniel's baseline level of fondness for Alex was already pretty ridiculous, and this ratcheted it up even higher.

He shut the door to the bedroom, then brushed his teeth and tried to take the world's quietest shower, because even though it might wake Alex up, Daniel felt fully disgusting after spending so long in an airplane. And, honestly, there was something about music festivals that made him feel itchy, like he needed about six showers and a flea dip to decontaminate, and two music festivals in two weeks was at least one too many.

When he stepped out of the shower, he found Alex at his kitchen table.

"Hey. Sorry to wake you," Daniel said, toweling his hair dry.

"I would have stayed at my own apartment if I wanted to sleep. You look good."

And that, Daniel supposed, was good to hear considering the fact that he was naked at the moment. "I missed you like crazy." They had spoken on the phone, but it obviously wasn't the same. "I'm so tired of talking to people who aren't you."

A little twitch of a smile worked at the corner of Alex's mouth. "Did you have dinner?"

"On the plane."

For a minute, Alex looked like he was going to take issue with this, but decided not to, probably remembering that Daniel usually had nothing more than a packet of saltines and some coffee grounds in his cabinet, and that a proper meal would have to wait until tomorrow.

"There are some pastries in the cupboard for your breakfast," Alex said. "Rogaliki from that place near my sister's house."

Daniel paused in tying the towel around his waist. He loved those fucking cookies. "Thank you." He took the two steps necessary to cross the room and bent to kiss Alex's cheek. "Thank you," he repeated. "It's so strange seeing you here. Good strange, though."

Alex yawned against Daniel's neck.

"Come on," Daniel said. "Bed." In the bedroom, he climbed directly into bed, not bothering with pajamas, but as he pulled up the sheets, he realized something was wrong. After two weeks in strange beds, he had almost forgotten what his own felt like, but he doubted it had ever felt this good.

"Alex," he said slowly. "Did you put your own sheets on my bed?"

"No, of course not," Alex said, his voice slightly muffled by the pillow. "I got you a set of your own. You always say my sheets are nicer."

"You got me new sheets?"

"Your old sheets are in a garbage bag near the door. And your old mattress is under the bed, in case you don't like this one."

"You got me a *mattress*?"

"Yours came with your apartment, Daniel," Alex said, scorn dripping from his voice. And, okay, Daniel's old mattress was pretty horrible and he had been meaning to replace it since about five minutes after moving in.

Daniel rolled back and forth and bounced a little, and sure enough, this mattress was amazing. "Come here." He tugged Alex's arm until he was half on top of Daniel and in kissing range. "Thank you." He kissed Alex then, not putting any particular heat into it because it was the middle of the night and Alex would have to wake up in a few hours to go to work, but Alex surprised him, bringing up a hand to cup his cheek and testing the seam of his mouth with his tongue.

Daniel instinctively shifted, moving a leg aside to make room for Alex, and kissed him back. He could feel Alex already hard against his thigh.

"Alex," he said, trying to suppress a burble of delighted laughter. "Did you come over because you were *horny*?"

"No! I needed to make sure you were in one piece."

Daniel slid his hand into the waistband of Alex's pajama pants, but Alex grabbed his wrist. "No—I want to try the thing. Tomorrow night."

It took Daniel a moment to catch up. "The thing" was making Alex come without anything touching his dick, and they had given it a few tries, but their efforts thus far had consistently been derailed when Alex started begging for Daniel to "just fuck me already." Daniel had never obeyed an order so quickly in his life.

"When was the last time you came?" Daniel asked, because they were operating on the theory that this would be easier if Alex hadn't come in a while.

"That night you were in town."

CHAPTER FOURTEEN

So, a week ago. "Poor you," Daniel said, meaning it.

"Yes, well. I spent my energy on acquiring bed linens instead."

"You sure you want to wait until tomorrow?"

"I'm afraid I'll fall asleep in the middle of it if we try now. But I can take care of you if you want." Alex had started saying that at some point in the last month—at first a little self-consciously and now almost offhand. Daniel was always careful not to not betray how fucking adorable he thought this was. Alex didn't go in much for deliberate sweetness—his instincts tended toward a sort of practical generosity with the people he cared about. Daniel needed a new mattress? Alex got him one. Mary needed time off? Alex covered her appointments as best he could.

But he didn't seem to view these actions as demonstrating anything. He didn't seem to think he had anything *to* demonstrate. He didn't buy sheets to show Daniel he cared; he bought Daniel sheets because they'd make Daniel happy. He had told Daniel exactly once that he loved him and then assumed Daniel didn't need reminding—which he didn't. He didn't use pet names and didn't engage in any behavior Daniel would describe as romantic. As Daniel didn't need or even especially want any of that, this suited him fine.

But this, the careful adoption of Daniel's phrase, was sweet, and deliberately so. Just now, Alex could have said "want me to blow you" or whatever, but instead he used Daniel's phrase. Daniel didn't exactly know why Alex did this, but he treated it as something eggshell fragile.

"I'll save it for tomorrow too," Daniel said now. "Let's sleep."

Alex was asleep almost as soon as his head hit the pillow,

Daniel following a few minutes later.

* * *

This was the third morning in the past week that Alex had to let himself into the clinic. Typically, Mary got there a full hour before her first appointment to review charts and just generally putter. Yesterday she had come in fifteen minutes *late*, full of apologies and looking like she'd been hit by a bus. One day last week she hadn't come in at all, and it had been Paul—Mary's husband, finally back in New York after his surgical residency ended earlier that summer—who called the office to let Alex know.

In anyone else, Alex would assume laziness, or even just a desire to finally spend time with her husband. But Paul worked even longer hours than Mary, and Mary had never been lazy a day in her life. She, like Alex, found ways to usefully fill what would otherwise be an empty hour. It was one of the reasons they had always gotten along: neither needed to prod the other to put in extra effort.

He knew, though, that this wasn't how most people operated; he used to think everybody else was lazy but now understood that he and Mary were outliers. Most people didn't want to work eleven-hour days; most people simply couldn't. Daniel always said he had at most four hours a day to give to The Man—Alex never pointed out that since Daniel freelanced, The Man was very literally himself, because this was probably not the point.

It was possible that Mary's schedule had just caught up to her. The summer had been grueling at the clinic: the elementary school year had finished up with a surprise outbreak of chickenpox that kept them both far too busy with sick visits. One of the nurses wound up catching it herself, which put the clinic into near chaos. For most of June, Alex left the clinic every evening feeling shattered, needing to spend at least an hour recovering before he could manage a conversation even with Daniel. It was early August now, though, and the clinic was at its slowest, but Mary only looked worse.

If she was finding her old pace to be too much, if it was wearing her down or just—Alex didn't know—making her sad, he wanted to know about it. He wanted to fix it.

So, at lunch when they were eating pork dumplings that Mary's mother-in-law had dropped off, steaming hot, he just asked her.

"Are you okay?"

"Yeah. I bitch about Paul's mother, but she's such a good cook. I ate twelve of these yesterday. Between her and my mother, I never have to make dinner anymore."

"I mean that you've been late a couple of times."

"People are late sometimes, Alex," she snapped.

He sighed. "I don't really care if you're late. Doctors are late all the time. I've never had to wait less than twenty minutes in a doctor's waiting room and I bet you haven't, either. We can just stop scheduling you before ten o'clock if that's what you need."

"Everything's fine, okay? We don't need to turn everything upside down."

"You look terrible."

"Wow. Thanks, friend." She shoveled a dumpling into her mouth in a distinctly aggressive manner.

Alex knew he was terrible at this. He usually relied on people to tell him if they needed something from him, and was never sure when asking personal questions crossed the line into being rude. He tried again, hoping he sounded concerned rather than annoyed. "Mary. I'm worried about you. Is there something wrong with your thyroid?" She had just eaten five jiaozi, hardly coming up for air. He was ready to drag her to an endocrinologist himself. And if it wasn't a thyroid problem, then it was worse: sudden exhaustion in an otherwise healthy young person was never good.

Something odd happened to her face. He was never the best at judging facial expressions, but over fifteen years of spending time with Mary meant he could usually figure her out. This was a new one, though.

"I really didn't want to tell you this," Mary said, and Alex's stomach lurched. Maybe she had already been to the doctor. Maybe she already knew what was wrong. "But I don't want you to worry. I'm pregnant."

"Oh," he said, torn between relief and confusion: relief that she wasn't sick, of course, and confusion about how to ask whether he was supposed to be happy or sad about it. He didn't know whether to offer congratulations or...

"It was on purpose, Alex," she said.

"Congratulations," he said, relieved to know what to say.

"It's really early. But I'm sick as a dog, so there's really no hiding it. My mother and Paul's mother both guessed and I wasn't going to lie to them. You can't eat half a pizza, throw up, and then go back and finish the pizza without people guessing, it turns out."

Well, that was going to put Alex off pizza for a while, but he supposed it was a good sign that Mary had an appetite, and he knew that morning sickness on its own wasn't dangerous. "How early?"

"Six weeks."

He paused. "So basically you did this as soon as Paul set foot in New York."

She started laughing and he guessed he had phrased that badly, but was there any other way to put it? He didn't think so. He knew how to count. "We should hire Linda Delgado two days a week," he said instead of trying to figure out where he had gone wrong. "That'll take some of the pressure off your schedule, and also we need a doctor who speaks Spanish."

They had been talking about this for over a year—Mary and Alex both spoke enough Spanish to treat a patient, but they had started this clinic to provide immigrant patients with care from doctors who shared their native language. There were other free or low-cost clinics in the city, but they didn't always make it easy to get continuing care from the same doctor or to find a doctor who spoke the patient's language. Dr. Delgado had been born in Puerto Rico, like so many people in the neighborhood. And she only wanted part time work, having retired from hospital practice.

"Ugh," Mary said. "I don't want to talk about it. I'm pregnant, not dying, and everyone says that morning sickness goes away after the first few months. Just give it time."

Alex very much wanted to point out that time might relieve Mary of morning sickness but instead she'd get a *baby*, which seemed even more of a scheduling difficulty. He shoved a potsticker into his mouth so he wouldn't be tempted to say this out loud.

Chapter Fifteen

"I know I'm being a giant baby," Alex said. He was having a full-on sulk into his empanada and kind of *was* acting like a baby, but it was pretty cute. "But why did she have to get pregnant already?"

"She's thirty," Daniel pointed out. "This isn't an unusual time to have a kid." He couldn't figure out if Alex's mixed feelings were due to worrying that the clinic would be thrown into an uproar, or because his childhood friend was becoming a mother, or for some other reason.

"So am I!" Alex said.

Daniel raised his eyebrows. "Are you sad that you aren't pregnant?"

"What is wrong with you?" Alex sputtered. But that was a definite smile happening on Alex's mouth, so Daniel was taking it as a win. "No, I am not jealous. I don't want that. We've had that conversation."

Indeed they had, mainly because Daniel had blurted the question out before he could think better of it. "You're allowed to feel sad about something not really being a possibility for us," he said now, tacking that *us* onto the end of the sentence because *you* sounded too much like Daniel was going to run off and get people pregnant in his spare time, and he was always going to err on the side of embarrassing himself rather than letting Alex think for one minute that he was anything less than fully, hopelessly committed.

"I don't, though," Alex said, and either the *us* hadn't registered for him or he took it for granted, and both of those explanations were fine by Daniel. "I don't want kids. I see kids all day. I'd be an adequate father, I know this, but that doesn't actually make me want to be one."

"So it's not that. What is it, then, that's bugging you?"

"It just seems so...adult."

This was, on the face of it, absurd. Alex was a doctor. He made a good living. He had a nice apartment and a wardrobe of boring but good-quality clothing. He had a savings account for his retirement. He took vitamins and thought about his sodium intake. He was easily as responsible as any adult Daniel knew, possibly even more so.

But Daniel had just spent two weeks surrounded by literal teenagers who were sleeping in vans for "the experience" and seemed to do nothing but listen to live music, use drugs that even Daniel felt suspicious about, and get sunburns. In upstate New York, he had looked out at the hundreds of thousands of people gathered in a field and thought: every one of these children is going to get crabs. By the time he left California, he didn't want to write a piece about the festivals so much as he wanted to write a pamphlet about basic hygiene and venereal disease. *Deodorant, Condoms, The Grateful Dead, and You* could be the title. *Stop Buying Drugs from Strangers* could be the subheading.

In other words, Daniel thought he understood the gut punch of a realization that you were as much of an adult as you were ever going to be.

"We're *adults*," Daniel commiserated. "I remember looking at people who thought about things like income tax and regular flossing and thinking: man, those fuckers don't know how to live. But that's me now. I'm the fucker."

It would have been really easy for Alex to point out that Daniel listened to music for a living and engaged in felony trespass as a hobby, that if you were trying to think of what a responsible adult looked like, it wouldn't be Daniel, with his too-long hair and his ripped jeans.

But Alex didn't say any of that. Instead he nodded. "Right? And I'm not even feeling nostalgic for some kind of wild youth. I didn't have one of those and didn't want to. I *like* being boring and predictable. But having a child—I don't know. This is *Mary*."

Daniel got it then: Alex was worried that Mary was ascending to some other plane of adulthood and leaving him. Maybe it was just the practical worry that Mary wouldn't have time for him; maybe it was more of an existential crisis. Maybe Alex didn't even know himself.

And there wasn't anything Daniel could say to reassure him, because people did often drop out of their old circles of friends after having kids. He didn't think that would happen with Mary—she and Alex had known one another for over half their lives. Alex was already very good at being an uncle and would find a place for himself in whatever Mary's life was like after she had kids.

"In a few months, you can probably talk Mary into letting you buy nursery furniture," Daniel said instead.

Alex visibly perked up at the prospect of being able to buy something both practical and expensive for his friend.

CHAPTER FIFTEEN

* * *

Whenever someone described Alex as being set in his ways, he bristled. He *was* set in his ways, but that was only because his ways were perfectly fine. He wasn't opposed to change—well, scratch that, he actually hated change—but the point was that he especially didn't care for change for change's sake. Once he found something worked, whether it be a style of checkbook or his regular order at his favorite Indian restaurant, he needed sufficient motivation to try something new.

But it had never occurred to him that having a consistent partner would change what he wanted in bed. He already had a good understanding of what he liked and felt comfortable doing, and this left him with a satisfactory amount of variety, and so he didn't think about it.

But after the first few weeks with Daniel, two things happened. One, it turned out that Daniel being interested in something was enough of a motivation for Alex to want to try it too. Two, things he had previously dismissed turned out to be worth a second thought when he contemplated doing them with a partner he trusted.

The first few times Daniel had fucked him, Alex had needed to be on top, because the only way he had ever enjoyed this was to maintain control. And it had been so good like that—Daniel sort of fiercely but dopily happy, his hands twisted in the bedsheets, making himself hold back. But then Alex had realized that his need for control was less of a pressing priority with Daniel. Maybe that was just because he knew Daniel would put Alex's comfort first, or maybe it was because sometimes Daniel realized Alex wasn't enjoying something even before Alex did.

That epiphany had ended with Alex being fucked over the back of the sofa, an excellent outcome for everyone concerned.

And now they were in Alex's bed, his new window air conditioner operating at enough of a hum to keep the muggy August heat at bay, Daniel kissing Alex with infuriating laziness.

"It's nice," Daniel protested when Alex objected.

"We had a plan," Alex pointed out.

"Yeah, and if you just wanted to come untouched you'd have done it with your dildo. You want to do it with me, so now you have to deal with me." But still, he reached for the lubricant and got to work.

Alex hadn't come in eight days, and at the first slick slide of Daniel's finger over his hole he already felt dangerously sensitive, like maybe they had gone about this all wrong. He was going to go off if Daniel looked at him the wrong way, never mind actually bothering with his prostate.

And then—"Oh fuck." The pad of Daniel's finger grazed that spot inside him and he remembered why he usually preferred to do this on his own. Not only did it take forever, but it made him desperate. He pushed into Daniel's touch.

"Shh," Daniel said. "I've got you."

Alex had always hated this, hated the vulnerability of being desperate—or, rather, of being the only desperate person in the room. Daniel was calm and collected, and he was in total control of Alex's reactions right now. Alex clapped a hand over his mouth because his noises only added to his embarrassment.

Daniel took Alex's hand away from his mouth and pressed a kiss to his palm.

"You're so pretty like this," Daniel said.

"Daniel," Alex complained.

"No, you really are, all pink and white. Making a mess of

yourself for me." He swiped a finger through the moisture on Alex's stomach, careful to steer clear of Alex's cock.

Alex groaned and couldn't have said whether it was from pleasure or embarrassment or some unholy combination of the two. His dick wouldn't stop leaking, and he knew—for fuck's sake, he was a doctor, he knew why it was happening. But when Daniel put it that way, it was mortifying and sweet and true: yes, Alex was making a mess of himself, and only for Daniel. The idea of doing this with anyone else was impossible.

"Roll over," Daniel suggested.

That only made it worse, of course, with his ass in the air, his cock leaking onto the sheets, not even able to see where Daniel was looking, and it somehow doubled how good he felt.

Daniel slid a second finger in, which wasn't necessary for this particular endeavor, and only served to make Alex want more. "You could fuck me," Alex said. Begged, really.

"Later. I promise. Right now we have a plan."

Alex felt Daniel's mouth at the top of his spine, pressing slow, wet kisses along the length of his back, all the while keeping up the maddening stroking inside him. He stopped at the base of Alex's spine, because that was the farthest Alex would let him go. He sucked a wet, open-mouthed kiss there, and it was low enough to trick Alex's body into thinking it was just a few inches lower still, and he felt the tension in his body gather closer, tighter.

"Daniel, please," he said. It was taking all Alex's effort not to reach for his erection.

"You're doing so good for me."

Alex felt himself tip over into a warm bath of pleasure, waves of orgasm washing over him so intensely that they blotted out everything else. He knew he was making noises but he didn't even care. He was vaguely aware of Daniel talking to him, but couldn't have separated his speech into separate words.

"Can I?" Daniel asked, and Alex finally understood.

"Please," Alex managed. When Daniel pressed into him it was so easy that Alex was almost embarrassed, for reasons he didn't quite understand. Daniel slid in with a groan, and wrapped a hand around Alex's still untouched erection, and Alex felt himself come again, sudden and shocking.

"Jesus Christ, Alex, did you just—"

Daniel was heavy and hot, draped across his back, one of his hands on Alex's shoulder and the other braced on the bed. It took what felt like a heroic effort for Alex to move one of his hands over to Daniel's. Daniel grasped it immediately—he always did, even when Alex was pretty sure all he had done was stretch out his fingers and think about how he'd like Daniel to hold his hand.

Afterward, when they were both was boneless and incoherent on the bed, Daniel's hand was still somehow touching his own.

Chapter Sixteen

Daniel would probably have liked Mr. and Mrs. Savchenko even if they hadn't been in the habit of showing him increasingly awful photographs of a surly, stone-faced teenage Alex.

There were no pictures from before Alex was about twelve, for reasons nobody alluded to or needed to explain, but after that, the Savchenkos evidently decided to make up for lost time by documenting all the most embarrassing moments in both their children's lives. There was Polyna, holding a cello and evidently dressed for a recital with hair that couldn't have been a good idea even in 1962. And there was Alex, gangly and with terrible skin, posed next to a microscope and a handmade poster about algae. The first time Daniel had seen this photograph, he had exclaimed something to the effect that it just figured Alex had to be beautiful even at his worst. Looking back, he had probably given the game away to both Mr. and Mrs. Savchenko at that point, even if it took Daniel longer to admit it to their son.

Daniel kind of adored Mr. Savchenko, who, despite his heavy accent and his refusal to drink American beer, was somehow the most aggressively typical American dad Daniel had ever met. He grilled in all weather. He kept up with every type of sport. He was a huge man who always greeted Daniel with a backslap and then, apparently thinking better of it, a giant hug.

Mrs. Savchenko was quiet, until someone made an effort to draw her out in conversation, which her husband did so gently that Daniel wasn't sure anyone even noticed it. She was plump and fair and looked like somebody's idea of a watercolor shepherdess, but she was a bookkeeper.

Polyna was a few years younger than Alex and somehow even prettier. She and her husband were both dentists. Their five-year-old son and an infant daughter had all the adults of the family wrapped around their little fingers.

At first Daniel had felt bad, thinking that they were all speaking English for his benefit, but it turned out that Polyna's husband only spoke English too.

Today it was hot, and somebody had set up a little inflatable pool on the tiny patio for Stepan while everyone else sat around in the shade, trying not to melt.

"We could be in my air-conditioned apartment," Alex muttered when Daniel passed him a beer from the cooler.

"You're just jealous that you can't go in the pool." But when nobody was looking, he briefly squeezed Alex's forearm, because he knew Alex had a hard time with these visits. Daniel didn't understand *why* Alex was so tense when seeing his parents, and when he asked Alex outright, all Alex said was that they all got on his last nerve, which seemed a typical enough family problem. Daniel loved his both his parents, but sometimes he reverted to sullen teenage obnoxiousness around them.

But Alex seemed—not precisely to enjoy seeing his family, but to enjoy having seen them. After the visit was over and he was safely at home, he'd start talking about it: his father ought to watch his sodium intake, Stepan was undoubtedly the smartest five-year-old to ever live, the baby has gotten so big.

Part of the problem had to be that, Alex's mother excepted, the Savchenkos were loud. They talked over one another. They shouted from room to room. Even with only eight people, one of whom was a baby who couldn't speak, there were somehow always at least three overlapping conversations. That number increased exponentially with every cousin, friend, neighbor, and colleague who visited. Alex could tolerate, maximum, one conversation at a time.

They all—at least Alex's parents and sister—knew what Daniel was to him, and probably had assumed as much before it was even true. Not that anyone said so out loud, of course. If Daniel had to guess, he'd say that none of them were quite comfortable with the idea of Alex being gay, but they liked that he had someone.

From the beginning, they had been scrupulously polite—not only polite, but warm—to Daniel. Maybe Mr. Savchenko was a little too deliberate with his backslaps and his hugs. Maybe Polyna made too painstaking an effort to ask Daniel about his work. But Daniel had been raised by a politician and a socialite and he knew that even premeditated kindness meant something, and in this case, it meant that Alex's family loved him and wanted him to be happy. Or maybe they just didn't want Alex to seize on rudeness to Daniel as a reason for him to stay away, which amounted to pretty much the same thing.

When Stepan, then three years old, had begun, unprompted, to call Daniel *uncle*, it had stuck. It had, Daniel always assumed, been too awkward for any of the adults to explain that *uncle* wasn't entirely accurate, and it was pretty impossible to argue with Stepan anyway, so the title had stuck. But Stepan's parents and grandparents never tried to correct him within Daniel's earshot, and never rolled their eyes or acted uncomfortable about it. They never acted uncomfortable about the fact of Daniel at all. Not acting uncomfortable was, Daniel knew, a pretty low bar to clear, but the world was filled with people who still didn't clear it.

"It's two o'clock," Alex said.

"He's probably looking for somewhere to park."

"There might have been traffic."

Daniel was confident there was plenty of traffic, but if his dad said he was going to be there at two, he'd be there at two. Around the tenth or eleventh time Dad had asked when he was going to meet Alex's family, Daniel had given in and asked Alex if it would be all right for his dad to stop by. Alex had responded in typical Alex fashion: honest bewilderment as to why Daniel's father wanted to meet his parents, and then continued bewilderment even after Daniel tried to spell it out for him.

It was Daniel's mother who had put it bluntly enough for Alex to understand. "He'd have met them if you were getting married," she said, and then, the next time she and Alex went out to lunch, she effectively kidnapped him and drove him to his parents' house so she could beat her ex-husband in the Meeting Alex's Family competition only she was engaged in.

Amazingly, Alex hadn't been put out by any of this—apparently Patricia Cabot was allowed to abduct him, and apparently the idea of being involved in something marriage-adjacent with Daniel wasn't horrifying to him.

The Savchenkos' doorbell rang and Mr. Savchenko dropped his tongs and his oven mitt and announced that he was getting the door and that nobody should try to get there first. Alex had told his parents that Daniel's father was going to be in Brooklyn for the day and wanted to see Daniel, which was the line Daniel had fed him, and which Daniel doubted any of the Savchenkos believed for a minute.

When Daniel made his way toward the front door, he found his father being enthusiastically interrogated by Mr. Savchenko about traffic, parking, whether it looked like a storm was coming, how he liked his burgers cooked, what he thought about the Mets' chances this season, and whether he wanted a beer. His dad responded with equal enthusiasm, handed over a bottle of wine and a houseplant, shook Alex's hand, and complimented Mrs. Savchenko on her home.

"Don't you look like an upstanding citizen, Dan," he said, reaching out to ruffle his hair.

"Ugh. Don't." Daniel ducked away. He always made an effort to look respectable for Alex's family, wearing what Alex called Businessman Drag, and which consisted of a pair of jeans with no holes and a shirt with a collar.

He was kind of surprised that Everett had stayed home, even though that had always been the plan: "We don't want to seem *generationally* queer," his dad had said. "At least not at first."

Daniel, who usually balked at anything resembling the closet, was willing to do what it took to make things easy for Alex. Sometimes he didn't notice how often he touched Alex until he spent an afternoon at a polite distance. Even before they were a couple, Daniel had kind of been all over Alex. But he had never needed to be told to rein it in in front of Alex's parents.

They ate burgers at a picnic table that almost seated all of them, while Alex's nephew threw a tantrum about the wrong kind of cheese on his burger, Alex's brother-in-law obligingly poured straight vodka into his wife's lemonade, and Alex and his mother sat at one end of the table, leaning towards one another as they talked about an article on plate tectonics they had read in *Scientific American.* Over all of this was a conversation about the upcoming mayoral election. Mr. Savchenko, apparently needing both hands to effectively communicate his feelings about the mayor, passed his granddaughter to Daniel, who proceeded to eat his burger with one hand.

It reminded Daniel, in a through-the-looking-glass sort of way, of summer dinners at his grandmother's house on Cape Cod, cousins having six conversations at once and adults doing pretty much the same thing, only with more alcohol. That was Daniel's frame of reference for what a normal family looked like. Even before his parents got divorced, he had never thought his nuclear family was anything like normal, with his father always traveling and his mother sometimes forgetting he was a child. His childhood had been good, just a little weird, but the Savchenkos had achieved television sitcom levels of ordinariness despite the fact that nearly all the adults had graduate degrees and the majority of people at the table had fled an oppressive regime at some point.

Throughout the meal, nobody acted like it was the slightest bit strange that Alex's friend's father was there.

Later, Daniel's dad gave them a lift back to the city, and Daniel didn't even have to explicitly say that Alex needed to be left alone in the back seat, undisturbed, the air conditioning operating at full blast.

"Thanks," Daniel said when they pulled up in front of Alex's building and Alex had gotten out of the car. He wasn't sure what he was thanking his father for, only that he was feeling a diffuse sense of gratitude and might as well let his dad know that he didn't actually resent his showing up that day.

"They like you."

"Was this—were you doing reconnaissance to make sure they liked me?" Daniel asked, faintly offended on behalf of the Savchenkos.

"No, but I thought they might just tolerate you and that you'd put up with it for Alex."

Daniel nearly protested, but it wasn't an unfounded concern. And the truth was that Daniel would indeed cheerfully put up with being outright mistreated by Alex's family if that was what Alex needed.

"I don't know if you caught it, but Mr. Savchenko got up from the table to get his camera."

"Yeah?" Daniel asked, confused as to why his father was mentioning it. Mr. Savchenko probably went through a roll of film a month just with snapshots of his grandchildren. Daniel doubted there were any children on the planet whose lives were as thoroughly documented as those two kids.

"He took a few of you and the baby," his father said before rolling up his window and driving away.

* * *

Despite having a weekend to rest, Mary only looked worse. She looked like she had lost weight, which shouldn't even have been possible given how much she was eating.

"You're not my doctor," she said when he told her as much, one afternoon as he rummaged through her desk looking for his favorite stapler. "And anyway, I throw up about half of what I eat."

"You might be dehydrated."

"You realize I'm a doctor too, right? And that I do know the signs of dehydration."

"You should call your doctor."

Mary didn't say anything, which was highly suspicious. She didn't even have the excuse of a mouth full of food.

"You don't have a doctor," he guessed.

"I have lots of doctors."

"But you don't have an obstetrician."

"I do," she said, but in a drawn-out way that he knew meant outright prevarication.

"You have a gynecologist, but you haven't been since missing a period," Alex guessed. He opened a desk drawer and found three staplers, which had to be two more than necessary, none of which was the one he was looking for. He put two of them in the pocket of his coat to return to the office manager.

"You know, this isn't a normal conversation to have with male colleagues, I'm sure of it. Besides, I did go in for a pregnancy test, so there. Look, I repeat, I am a doctor. There is nothing another doctor can do right now other than confirm that yes, I'm pregnant, and no, I'm not bleeding or cramping, and that I have a shitty case of morning sickness but nothing so bad that I need IV fluids."

"What does Paul—"

"Back off, Alex."

"Sorry, sorry," he said, not entirely sure what he had done wrong but shutting up anyway. He sorted the pens in the cup on her desk, throwing out the ones that had been chewed on or didn't have any ink left.

"Male colleague," he said a few minutes later. "*Male colleague?*"

"I nearly said 'man friend' but—"

"Jesus, no."

CHAPTER SIXTEEN

"Exactly."

Alex picked up some charts that Mary had finished and tucked them under his arm. Her desk nearly looked organized now.

"Want to hear the worst part?" she asked as he reached the door.

"Sure," he said, thinking he was either about to hear about a gross symptom or—worse—something emotionally complicated.

"Paul's mother got me this horrible tea from her acupuncturist and I think it's actually working. I only threw up once this morning."

Alex was not going to ask her if she had checked the ingredients to make sure none were contraindicated in pregnancy. She was, as she had reminded him twice, a doctor. And so was the acupuncturist, for that matter. "And this is bad, why?"

"Because she was right, and now she's going to foist horrible teas on me—and my children—for the rest of her life."

"I seem to remember you giving me horrible tea when I used to get headaches." It had been bitter and disturbing-tasting even after Alex doctored it with honey, and he couldn't be sure whether it actually worked—what worked was remembering to get enough sleep, which at the beginning of his residency had been a challenge. But he had dutifully drunk the tea anyway.

"Yes, but I actually like you."

"I hate to point this out, but Paul's mother could have just let you be sick. She didn't have to give you tea."

"I can't believe you're on her side," she griped.

"I'm always on your side," he said sincerely. But then he thought about it. "She cooks for you. She cleans your apartment. She keeps *your* mother busy so she doesn't harass you about losing weight or doing something with your hair or whatever your mother's latest problem with you is. She packs lunch for both of us sometimes. I kind of love your mother-in-law."

She sighed and slumped in her chair. "Oh please. You and Mrs. Cabot are as thick as thieves. You win the mother-in-law contest."

"She never cooks for me," Alex pointed out, rather than arguing that Patricia wasn't his mother-in-law, because that obviously wasn't the point.

Mary gave him an unimpressed look that she ruined with a yawn.

"Come on," he said. "I'm putting you in a cab."

"It's a ten-minute walk."

"Cab." He hauled her to her feet and out the door, neatly leaving the charts and staplers on the office manager's desk.

Chapter Seventeen

"I was going to drive up to see my grandmother next Friday," Daniel said. They had walked up to the Second Avenue Deli for lunch. Alex didn't have a one o'clock appointment, so they were lingering over crusts of rye bread and bottles of soda.

"Oh," Alex said, looking unaccountably disappointed, far more disappointed than anyone ought to be who had been spared the ordeal of seeing Daniel's grandmother. "I can't go."

Daniel had already known that. Alex didn't have a Friday off until just before Labor Day, and driving to Cape Cod on Labor Day weekend was about the worst idea Daniel could think of. But he hadn't expected Alex to go with him this time anyway.

"You won't be missing much," Daniel said.

"I didn't think I would be. I just thought you might like the company."

"Well, of course I would have."

"Then leave Saturday and come back Sunday, and I'll come with you."

"You really don't need to. Anyway, the traffic will be a million times worse if we do it that way."

Daniel didn't think about that conversation until he was getting ready to leave on Friday morning.

"Call me when you get there," Alex said as they stood on the sidewalk outside his building, Alex getting ready to head to work and Daniel about to walk up to Union Square for the subway to Penn Station.

"It'll be the middle of the afternoon," Daniel pointed out.

"Do phones in Massachusetts not work in the afternoon?" Alex snapped.

"I meant that you'll be with patients."

"Leave a message, Daniel."

"I wasn't planning *not* to call you. I just would have called you at home tonight. I wasn't going to go the whole weekend without calling you." Daniel didn't even know why he felt like he had to point this out. First, he wasn't even going to be away the entire weekend, only until the following night. Second, he had never called Alex from his grandmother's house before. Previously, it hadn't even occurred to him as a thing he ought to do, but now that they were together, he had assumed he'd check in with Alex at some point during the two days he'd be away.

"I want to know sooner rather than later that you aren't dead on the side of the road," Alex said, sounding distinctly pissy about it.

"Are you mad that I'm doing something alone?" Daniel asked, utterly confused. Daniel did things on his own all the time; he had been out with Lauren and Jacob twice in the last week and gone to see a movie with Jacob the previous week. He saw Blanca and Miriam nearly every afternoon. Alex knew about all of this.

Alex looked like he'd been slapped. "No. Christ. I'm the last person to fault you for that. But do you prefer to make this trip alone?"

Daniel didn't know how to answer that. "Yes" would be a lie, but "no" wasn't quite right, either. It had been much more pleasant with Alex there, but he wanted to spare Alex the ordeal. He couldn't say which he preferred without qualifiers.

While he was ruminating over his answer, Alex rolled his eyes, squeezed Daniel's shoulder, and went to work.

Daniel repeated that conversation to himself again and again as he got mired in exactly the sort of traffic he ought to have expected on a Friday in August, traffic jams for some reason always coinciding with dead spots on the road that didn't pick up radio signals from either Boston or Hartford.

It wasn't unusual for Alex to be in a bad mood, but it was unusual for that bad mood to be directed at Daniel, and it was even more unusual for Daniel not to know what had precipitated the bad mood. Obviously, it had something to do with this trip, but he couldn't figure out what.

When he arrived, he hugged Magda and called the clinic from the extension in the kitchen. Alex was with a patient, so Daniel left a message with the receptionist. He had no idea what the receptionist must think about Daniel leaving a message informing Dr. Savchenko that his friend arrived safe and sound. He might as well have just outed Alex on the spot, which was something Alex probably hadn't thought of when he asked Daniel to leave a message.

That night, his grandmother seen to, the annual visit to the lawyer accomplished, and Magda and the nurse both repeatedly assured that Daniel and his father would provide references in the event that Mrs. Cabot fired them, Daniel called Alex at home.

"Did you eat dinner?" Alex asked immediately, so Daniel guessed that whatever he had done, he was forgiven.

"Magda made me pierogi. They weren't like the kind we get at Vaselka or the kind your mom makes, but they were really good."

"She made you pierogi," Alex said flatly.

"She thought you'd be coming too," Daniel explained.

"Did she." There was something in Alex's voice that hovered between amusement and annoyance. "Why do you think she assumed that?"

"I think we were probably pretty obvious when we were here last time. I mean, we weren't together yet, but I guess the fact that I brought you at all made her think we were."

Alex was silent for a moment. "I was beginning to think I was out of line in thinking that you ought to have asked me to come, but now that I know Magda's on my side, this changes everything."

Daniel wished he could see Alex's face, because he was about eighty percent sure he was joking but couldn't know for certain without seeing whether his mouth was doing that twitch it got when he thought he was funny. "Are you mad that I didn't invite you to spend seven hours in traffic and then get called a degenerate by my grandmother?"

"Yes."

"*Why?*"

"Why do you think? Because you're sad and you hate being sad and alone."

Daniel opened his mouth to protest, but then realized it would have been a lie. "I...yeah. Okay. A little. But not because of my grandmother."

"No?"

"It's the house. It's too quiet. It was always filled with people and now I don't know where half those people even are. It's so weird to think that I used to have a big family and now I don't." Then it occurred to him that he probably shouldn't complain about this to someone who had left his grandparents and cousins on the other side of the Iron Curtain. "It's really not a big deal, though. I don't think about it unless I'm here."

"I have a hard time walking past the apartment where I lived with my parents for the first few years after we came here," Alex said.

"The one on 7th? We walk past it all the time."

"*We* walk past it, but I don't. Not by myself. It's just too weird a feeling. Not bad, just unsettling. Like my brain gets cluttered up with old memories that I didn't ask for. But when you're around—I don't know. You're a reminder that things turned out fine for the boy who lived in that apartment."

That was probably more than Daniel had ever heard Alex say about that period of time. "And you wanted to do that for me," he asked, his voice sounding small and hopeful, as if he needed reassurance about something he already knew.

"Yes, Daniel," Alex sighed. "It seems like something you should be able to count on me for."

"Is this one of those things that's different now that we're..." In person, Daniel usually filled in the absent word in this sentence with a vague gesture in the space between the two of them. Over the phone, he didn't know what to do. "Together," he finally said.

"I don't know," Alex said slowly. "I don't think so? You should be able to lean on someone for the things that are hard for you, or even just day-to-day annoyances. And when someone you care about—even just a friend—is sad, I think it's normal to want them to feel better if that's within your power. I don't think there's anything specifically romantic about that, but it's something I've thought about more since we've been together."

Daniel wondered what it meant that "together" rolled off Alex's tongue like that, like he was comfortable assuming all the things that were baked into that word and didn't need to second guess any of it. Maybe Daniel could stop thinking about it too.

"I think that when you see someone every day," Alex went on, his pace measured and thoughtful, as if he were weighing his words, "when you have them in the back of your mind when you're making plans or buying groceries or whatever, it's—a life. At that point you're having a life together, you've already made choices that tie your lives up together, and it makes sense for the serious things, the sad things, to be a part of that."

Daniel wasn't sure he'd put it exactly that way. He couldn't remember ever making the choice to enmesh his life with Alex's; it had been a thousand little blink-and-you-miss-it decisions, and it made his skin crawl to think that everything could have been different if he just hadn't brought Alex those donuts that one time or if he hadn't invited himself along to visit Alex's family.

Usually, with any kind of remotely difficult conversation, Daniel preferred to have it face-to-face, especially with Alex. He wanted as many points of contact as possible, preferably with him pressed along Alex's side. But tonight Alex had said more to him than he usually did. Alex usually kept phone conversations short, only long enough to establish where and when to meet. But maybe the telephone let Alex imagine he wasn't talking to a person, or at least not get distracted by the fact. Maybe it was easier for Alex, not having to see Daniel's face, just speaking into the ether. Daniel would make sure to remember that.

"A life," Daniel said now, mortified to hear how shaky he sounded. "Yeah. That's—that's definitely how I think of it too. Are we okay?"

"Daniel. We were okay before we even talked."

* * *

Alex came home from the grocery store to find Daniel already in his apartment, his overnight bag and shoes strewn haphazardly by the front door.

"There must have been no traffic at all," Alex said after dropping his groceries on the counter. It wasn't even three o'clock.

Daniel letting himself in when Alex wasn't home was a new thing, and Alex liked it too much to dare draw attention to it.

"I left really early," Daniel said, coming up behind Alex and hooking his chin over Alex's shoulder. Daniel's hair was wet and he smelled like Alex's soap, so he may just have wanted to take a shower in a bathroom that wasn't a health hazard and so had stopped by before going home. Or maybe he had realized he had no food or clean clothes at his apartment—Alex's laundry had been coming back with some of Daniel's mixed in for months now, and Alex simply placed it all in the drawers he had cleared out to store Daniel's things.

"You going out tonight?" He could feel Daniel shake his head. "I got ingredients for that chicken thing you like. Or we can go to the new Indian restaurant that you wanted to try." Every time a new restaurant opened in the neighborhood, Daniel had to try it. It was pathological. The sane approach was obviously to wait and see if they were still open in three months, maybe look into their health code violations.

"Don't care," Daniel mumbled into Alex's neck.

Or maybe Daniel had come over for other reasons. That seemed likely, judging by the way he was mouthing at Alex's jaw and trailing a hand under his shirt.

Alex pretended to ignore him, stacking cans in the cabinet and putting beer on the refrigerator door even as Daniel bit his shoulder, even as he scratched a fingernail over the tip of one nipple.

This was Daniel wanting attention, and Alex was going to give him all the attention he wanted, and then some, and they both knew it.

"Do you want a snack?" Alex asked, biting back a smile when Daniel whined. "Something to drink?" Daniel unzipped Alex's pants. "Maybe there's something on television that you'd—" He had to stop to collect himself when Daniel slid a hand inside his pants. "Or maybe we could go see Mary. Yes, that's the plan. You haven't seen one another in days. Or—I know—do you want to call your mom and see if—"

That must have been Daniel's breaking point, because he pushed Alex against the wall. "You're so mean," he said, laughter in his voice. He kissed just inside the open collar of Alex's shirt before Alex pulled him up for a proper kiss. Daniel tasted like Alex's toothpaste, not the stuff with cartoon characters on the packaging that he had at his own apartment.

They managed to get to the bedroom. Light spilled across the covers, and all Alex wanted was to see Daniel there, spread out on the clean sheets.

"You want anything in particular?" Alex asked when he got

CHAPTER SEVENTEEN

Daniel where he wanted.

Daniel shook his head.

In this mood, Daniel not having a preference meant "anything goes as long as it ends with me being railed into the mattress," which was more than fine by Alex.

And—the fact that Alex knew that, the fact that he could look at Daniel and understand the thoughts inside his head, felt like a minor miracle. It was often hard enough to understand what other people meant when they used their words. But he knew Daniel well enough, knew what it meant when he was quiet, knew what it meant when he was chatty. The subtle shifts of his body language made more sense to Alex than entire sentences from other people.

Alex was fluent in two languages, conversational in another two, and could stumble along in a couple more, and nothing made as much sense to him as being in the same room as Daniel. And it worked both ways: sometimes Alex didn't need to utter a syllable in order for Daniel to understand him, didn't have to sift through his thoughts and try to assemble them into words, a task that was sometimes just this side of impossible.

He peeled off Daniel's clothing and laid it over the chair in the corner of the room whose sole purpose was to catch clothing that Daniel couldn't yet commit to the laundry hamper, for reasons Alex didn't understand.

"You've been getting sun," Alex said, running a finger across Daniel's biceps, along the line where his T-shirt usually ended. All summer, Alex had been watching freckles materialize out of thin air and land on Daniel's shoulders and the bridge of his nose. He had watched Daniel's hair lighten from a warm chocolate to something so streaky that it that defied categorization. And in a month or two he'd watch the process reverse itself, freckles disappearing, hair fading back to normal.

It felt so intimate—except maybe *intimate* wasn't the word, because those signs were there for the world to see. But knowing someone well enough to predict these changes, and knowing he'd be around to see it all for himself, felt like a different kind of intimacy, even though it boiled down to something as mundane as knowing for sure that this person would be around tomorrow.

And Daniel *would* be around tomorrow—Alex knew he could count on that. He could count on something more concrete than Daniel simply being around, but wasn't sure he could put it into words. He had gotten close the previous day when he had told Daniel that he wanted them to have a life together.

In the mail a few days earlier, there had been an envelope from Alex's father, containing a few snapshots from the last time Alex and Daniel had visited. Daniel's father habitually got photographs developed in duplicate and gave half to Polyna, because most photographs had her children in them, after all. But this batch of snapshots had been of Daniel and Alex's niece. Larysa had been asleep on Daniel's shoulder, her mouth hanging open and her hands balled up into fists in Daniel's shirt.

It wasn't the first time Daniel had held the baby, but it was the first picture Alex had of it, and he already knew he'd be keeping this photo, sliding it into a frame that he'd probably put on his desk at work. Or maybe he'd keep it at home and tuck it away someplace safe where he could look at it when he needed a reminder that Daniel was his as much as the baby was, as much as his sister was, and that Alex wasn't the only one who knew it.

Daniel closed his eyes and seemed to sink further into the

mattress. Alex pushed at his shoulder until he rolled onto his stomach, then ran a hand over his upper back. Just as he had suspected, his shoulders and neck were tense. Part of it was from working in the garden, but the rest was likely from holding himself stiff while stuck in traffic. Alex straddled Daniel's hips, then dug his thumbs into a knot in his trapezius. Daniel groaned.

"Too much?" Alex asked.

"In a good way. Keep going."

"This is all from driving," Alex said, trying to work that knot out. "None of this was there the other day."

"Probably," Daniel mumbled.

Alex leaned over and opened the nightstand drawer, pulling out a bottle of almond oil he had gotten at the health food store a few weeks back, thinking it would be a decent middle ground been spit and Vaseline, and also that it wouldn't taste as horrible as Vaseline. But it would work for this too. He poured some in his palm and then rubbed his hands together before smoothing them over Daniel's back.

"I'm going to learn to drive," Alex said. The idea had occurred to him when talking with Daniel on the phone yesterday, and the prospect still only seemed mildly horrifying, so he was going to do it.

Daniel made an inquisitive noise into the pillow.

"That way you don't have to drive the entire way."

"You don't have—"

"Stop. We've had this conversation and it was boring the first time."

Daniel halfheartedly attempted to swat Alex, blindly waving a hand behind his back. "You'll go fifty-five miles an hour and obey all traffic regulations," he mumbled. "We'll never get out of Connecticut."

Alex didn't know how long he spent rubbing Daniel's back, or when it was that he felt Daniel go lax beneath his hands. But when he whispered Daniel's name and got no response other than a shallow, regular breath, Alex carefully climbed off the bed and pulled a blanket over Daniel's sleeping body.

* * *

Daniel woke up to the feeling of fingers sifting through his hair. He turned just enough to see Alex, sitting up against the headboard and reading a magazine.

"I was just trying to decide whether to wake you up," Alex said, still playing with Daniel's hair.

"What time is it?" He could also have asked what day it was. He was pretty sure it was still Saturday, and that he had woken up that morning in Cape Cod, but it was possible that a night had passed and it was already Sunday.

"It's four. You were only out for an hour."

Daniel didn't know how to feel about the fact that he had arrived unannounced at Alex's apartment, attempted to get him into bed, and then passed out. He hadn't even thought that he was tired, but Alex's hands on his stupid aching back had been like some kind of off switch.

"My back feels great," Daniel said, stretching. "All of me feels pretty great." Then he got onto his knees and swung a leg over Alex's lap. Alex tossed the magazine onto the nightstand and settled his hands on Daniel's hips.

He tasted like he had made himself tea while Daniel slept, and Daniel kissed him like he was trying to lick the honey out of Alex's mouth. He had woken up loose-limbed and half hard, and now he wanted to finish what they had started earlier.

Alex was still mostly dressed, wearing his undershirt and pants. Daniel rolled to the side to take off the rest of his clothes and watched Alex do the same.

Sometimes, when they had nowhere to be and neither of them were tired, they could spend the better part of an afternoon making out like teenagers. Daniel thought that was where this was heading, but Alex surprised him by rolling him onto his back and sliding down the bed.

At some point over the past few months, Alex had figured out everything that Daniel wanted in a blowjob, and then gave it to him all at once in a way that fried every nerve cell in Daniel's body. Sometimes he was relentless about it, making Daniel come hard and fast, knowing that Daniel could usually get hard again pretty soon.

But now he was flicking his tongue along the length of Daniel's shaft, teasing little licks that made Daniel wonder where the hell he picked that trick up, because he didn't have it three months ago. Then he sucked too gently on the tip of Daniel's cock—more teasing.

"You okay with being fucked?" Alex asked.

Daniel nodded enthusiastically. "Please."

Alex pushed at Daniel's knees, a signal to bend them, and Daniel complied. And then—Jesus Christ, Alex began sucking on one of his balls.

Daniel let one of his hands fall on Alex's head—not pushing or even guiding, just a point of contact, and shut his eyes, giving himself over to what was happening, knowing that Alex would make it good. There was a finger sliding over his hole, a warm, wet tongue flicking over the underside of his erection, a hand somehow in his own.

"I could come like this," he said.

"Do you want to?" It seemed like a trick question, so Daniel didn't answer. "Or can I fuck you."

"Yes, that," Daniel said immediately. "But let me suck you first. Just a little."

"If you insist," Alex said, sounding ragged and amused.

He rolled halfway onto his side and gestured for Alex to sit up. This might not work, he had never tried it, but he sure as hell had thought about it. He slicked up his fingers with the almond oil, then pulled one of his legs up and reached behind himself, which was how he liked to do this to himself. Then he braced himself on an elbow and bent over to take Alex's cock into his mouth.

"You don't have any leverage," Alex said. But Daniel didn't think he needed leverage—what he needed was Alex's cock in his mouth and his own fingers in his ass, and that's what he had. He wasn't doing a brilliant job at either task, but it felt good. He felt...full, maybe, and a little obscene, knowing he was on display like this.

Alex shifted and did something with one of his legs so Daniel was more comfortable, then reached down and palmed Daniel's ass.

"You look..." Alex said, but he didn't finish the sentence. He didn't need to. Daniel could tell from the twitch of Alex's cock in his mouth that he was enjoying this. Alex could probably slide one of his one fingers in alongside Daniel's, could do that to Daniel's mouth too.

Daniel pulled off, gasping. "I was too close." Another minute and the friction of the sheet against his dick would have sent him over the edge.

Alex moved aside carefully, so Daniel's head was no longer

in his lap. "Don't move," Alex said, and Daniel didn't, instead feeling Alex shift beside him and behind him. He heard the sound of the Vaseline cap being unscrewed, metal against glass, then felt the blunt pressure of Alex against him. He was still mostly on his side, with one knee up against his chest, and—oh god—Alex pushing into him.

Like this, he could hardly move. All he could do was take it, and just the thought of that sent sparks flying down his spine.

He'd been in a mood since yesterday, maybe even the day before. It happened from time to time, and wasn't what he'd call a bad mood, just the strange sense that his feelings were a size too big for his skin. That non-fight with Alex, followed by Alex saying all those nice things, the hours in traffic, and the predictable awfulness of his grandmother and that echoing empty house—there was too much in his head and his heart for Daniel to be there too. Which probably made no sense, but that didn't stop it from happening anyway. He could usually wait out these moods or put some of that restless energy to good use in the garden. Pot sometimes took the edge off. A different kind of person might have taken up sports, but Daniel was very much not that kind of person.

He had never thought about sex as a way to cope with that particular mood, maybe because usually he focused on what made his partner feel good, and that meant being—present, he supposed. Aware. Very in his head. Usually, making people feel good was what did it for him, to the point that Daniel was pretty sure it was a *thing*.

But like this, with Alex, he could just take. Because *take*, in this context, meant *let*. He was letting Alex do what he pleased, taking pleasure inside Daniel's body, and there was nothing Daniel could do except let him. He didn't need to think, he didn't need to move—he could just give himself up to what was happening.

He was making nonsense noises into the pillow, Alex's mouth at the nape of his neck, one of Alex's arms around his chest to keep him in place. And Alex—God—Alex was murmuring nonsense in return. Just things like "it's all right" and "I have you," which told Daniel all he needed to know about how desperate he was acting, and that, for some reason, only ratcheted up his need.

Alex shifted in a way that Daniel, by now, recognized as Alex pulling back enough to look at him. It always made him feel self-conscious, like he didn't know whether to hide or flex or what. Now he felt Alex's palm on his ass, spreading him a little, and—okay, he was watching his own cock in Daniel's ass. This wasn't the first time he had done that, but it was the first time he slid a finger in alongside his cock.

The stretch was almost too much. It was—unprecedented, some voice in Daniel's addled brain supplied. It was certainly more than he was used to.

"This okay?" Alex asked.

Daniel nodded into the pillow.

"I need words."

"Don't stop."

Alex didn't stop. He pushed that finger in and twisted it, finding the place he was looking for and making Daniel moan into the pillow. He was going to be sore tomorrow. Alex would feel bad about it, would stroke an apologetic finger down his crease, across his swollen rim, and—fuck, he was really close. Between the extra fullness and the thing Alex was doing with his fingertip, he was on the brink. He didn't want to come yet, though; he wanted to drag this out, stay poised on the edge.

CHAPTER SEVENTEEN

He had needed this, had needed something to shake loose the weirdness of his mood, something to remind him that he was his body as much as he was his mind. He'd come in ten seconds if he could get a hand around his dick, but the way he was arranged, that wasn't a possibility, and both Alex's hands were busy. Alex was hardly thrusting anymore, just letting Daniel grind back as much as this position would allow, his breath hot and ragged on Daniel's neck. He had the feeling this could stretch out infinitely, both on the brink of climax, neither going anywhere, suspended indefinitely.

"Hands and knees," Daniel gasped when it became too much, and then Alex was thrusting into him, a little too hard, his rhythm shaky and desperate, everything about it completely perfect. It took only the most glancing contact with his dick to push Daniel over the edge, and the only thing that prevented him from collapsing into the mattress was the hand on his hips. Alex followed him over almost immediately.

Neither of them said anything for a while, Alex probably because he was out of breath, and Daniel because he was in a stupor.

"Shower," Alex said. "Or we'll regret it."

"Your sheets regret it," Daniel mumbled, which made no sense but was still accurate.

They really didn't both fit into Alex's shower, but that hadn't stopped them so far and probably wasn't going to stop them in the future. And this wasn't even a sexy shower—they were both fucked out and tired, neither managing much more than leaning against one another and halfheartedly doing things with soap.

Daniel noticed that there was a new bottle of shampoo in here that hadn't been on the ledge when he'd showered earlier. It was the brand he used himself, which meant Alex had picked it up at the grocery store. Daniel had been meaning to bring a bottle over, but kept second-guessing himself, like a bottle of shampoo in Alex's apartment would somehow be more intrusive than the fact that Daniel himself was there almost every night and every morning.

They changed the sheets and got dressed—or at least Alex got dressed, while Daniel put on jeans and left it at that.

"Do you want to try that new Bangladeshi restaurant?" Daniel asked.

"Okay," Alex said, managing to sound indulgent about it, as if he hadn't been systematically ranking beef shatkora at every Bangladeshi restaurant in the neighborhood, primly explaining to Daniel that ordering the same dish every time was the scientific method, Daniel, it is not my fault if you don't appreciate scientific inquiry. He always wound up eating half Daniel's biryani anyway.

"Sounds good," Daniel said, and went to find a clean shirt.

Chapter Eighteen

"She's not the same as you," Alex said.

"It would be strange if she were," Mary pointed out.

"But is she good?"

"She's good," Alex said. "But you were there too. What did you think?"

They had brought Dr. Delgado in for a trial run during the hectic end-of-summer period when parents realized they needed to schedule back-to-school physicals and get minor problems dealt with before school started. Dr. Delgado was older than both Mary and Alex, but didn't act like her extra experience meant she was everybody's boss. She was kind to the office staff, great with children, and patient with parents.

"She's good," Mary said. "I just hate the idea of hiring anyone else."

"Realistically, you'll be taking a few days off when the baby is born, Mary. There's no way around that."

Mary rolled her eyes. This was her least favorite topic, because she seemed to be under the impression that nothing was going to change after this child was born. And maybe it wouldn't—Alex didn't know. But it seemed wise to prepare for the—not the worst, because Mary cutting back on hours wasn't *bad*, per se, it was just...

It was bad. The idea of Mary not being at the clinic full time was awful. Alex hated it. He could make peace with the idea of Mary being a mother, of there being an entire extra human present when he saw her and Paul—and he was aware that this was a shitty way to anticipate the arrival of a baby, but it wasn't like Alex would actually ever say any of this to Mary. But Mary not being at the clinic at all wasn't something he could bring himself to think about.

He hadn't told her this. Nothing would compel him to admit any of this out loud, because she had enough to think about without his feelings being added to the mix.

But that was getting ahead of himself. "She only wants two days a week," he said, "but she's willing to work full time while you're on leave. Everything after that, we deal with later." But some of his anxiety must have been obvious, because Mary frowned at him.

"Alex," she said. "I have two middle-aged Chinese women living in my apartment. I don't need to stay home with this baby. I don't want to stay home with this baby. I might want to work shorter days, but I don't know yet. This clinic is mine just as much as it is yours, and I'm not walking away from it."

"Okay," Alex said.

"And even if I did—which isn't happening—I'd still be around. You get that, right? I'm not vanishing off the face of the earth. I'd still be your friend even if we didn't work together."

Alex supposed he knew that, theoretically, but they had never put it to the test. They had gone to high school together, then college and medical school together (and if the fact that Alex followed Mary around like a lost dog for a decade was weird, she had never said so, and so Alex was determined not to think of it as weird). Even though they had separate residencies, they had been very much going through the same things at the same time. This would potentially be the first time they hadn't had that sense of common purpose.

But there was nothing Alex could do about that, and telling Mary that he had his doubts would only make things worse, so he let out a breath. "Okay. Do we know if Dr. Delgado is, uh, okay with…" He gestured vaguely at himself. "Queer people?"

It was tricky—in this neighborhood, being gay was relatively unremarkable, but medicine was conservative, pediatrics especially so. Plenty of parents would never take their kids to a gay pediatrician. So Alex wasn't completely out at work, but he also wasn't closeted. One of the nurses was a lesbian, and she knew Alex was gay. The receptionist had proudly announced that her grandson marched in the pride parade last summer, and if she had made this announcement after noticing that Daniel came to pick Alex up after work most days, she didn't mention it outright. He was pretty sure the entire office staff gossiped and had come to some perfectly correct opinions about him and Daniel, but since they still worked at the clinic and there hadn't been an exodus of patients, he assumed they could keep their mouths shut when they needed to.

But he really didn't want to work with a bigot.

"Oh, I just asked her," Mary said. "She's fine. I told her that we both did our residencies in places with a large population of indigent homosexual teenagers and we feel strongly about gay rights. She said she was on board and mentioned the usual lesbian sister-in-law."

Alex snorted. He had heard about more gay sisters-in-law (and cousins, therapists, neighbors, and uncles) than he could count. "You know, my aunt is a lesbian," was apparently shorthand for "I noticed that you seem gay and here's proof that I'm fine with that."

"Thanks," Alex said. And then something Mary had said a few minutes earlier struck him. "Are you going to get a bigger apartment?" There was no way four adults and a baby could live in Mary's two-bedroom apartment on Hester Street. He honestly wasn't sure how four adults and a baby could live anywhere. But Mary seemed unbothered by that aspect of the arrangement, and even seemed to have warmed to Paul's mother a little.

It occurred to Alex that it likely wouldn't only be four adults—Mary's younger brother came and went. Alex had no idea where Simon was now, and doubted that Mary did, either.

"We've been looking," Mary said. "There's no such thing as a four-bedroom apartment, apparently, and we're not moving out to Queens, I don't care what my mother thinks. Paul likes the idea of a loft, but when I think about how much our mothers would have to say about exposed ductwork, I don't think I could take it."

"You could get a loft on Spring Street for fifteen thousand or so," Alex said. "Over two thousand square feet. You could pay someone to hide the ducts."

"That's exactly what Paul says."

Alex had looked at a few SoHo lofts himself, more from curiosity than anything else. He didn't want to live that far from the East Village. A few years ago, the city had legalized converting vacant warehouses to residential lofts, but only in SoHo. The dozens of former warehouses in the vicinity of Astor Place and the Bowery were either empty or filled with people doing illegal loft conversions.

"The building next to mine is going co-op," Alex said. "A two-bedroom is ten thousand dollars."

"What does it say that I'd consider buying two two-bedroom apartments and knocking a wall out? Is that crazy?"

Alex's experience was that it was impossible to discuss Manhattan real estate without sounding crazy in one way or another.

"Wait," Mary said. "Why are you paying all this attention to real estate? Are you planning to buy something?"

"My lease is up this fall." Alex had lived in the same apartment since finishing medical school. It was fine for one person, or for two people who didn't mind being in one another's hair, but with Daniel there so often, they were always having to step around each other. Also, he kind of just wanted to own something, even if the precarious New York housing market meant that buying something could mean effectively throwing his money away. He wasn't leaving the city; he wasn't even leaving the neighborhood. This had been his home since he'd arrived in his country and it was staying that way. It didn't really matter if property values plummeted, because he wouldn't be selling.

"What does Daniel think?" Mary asked.

And that was the crux of the problem. Or, not a problem, really, but a consideration. If he bought an apartment, he'd be doing it with Daniel in mind: he'd find somewhere near enough to Daniel's horrible apartment, and also somewhere near tempting vacant lots that Daniel might want to get his hands on. Realistically, Daniel would wind up spending a significant amount of time at whatever apartment Alex bought. Alex could just buy an apartment and tell Daniel about it, but he thought he ought to tell Daniel first, that way he could have a say.

It was possible that Daniel would want more than a say. They hadn't discussed living together, except in the inverse: they both liked having their own space. But lately the fact that they liked their own space had been pretty irrelevant because they were with one another practically all the time. If Daniel wanted to move in, Alex would welcome it—in a larger apartment.

But Alex didn't want to ask Daniel, because he was afraid Daniel would give him the answer he thought Alex wanted.

* * *

The tail end of August wasn't the best time to break ground on a new garden, but Daniel told himself he wasn't so much breaking ground as clearing the plot of health hazards. This lot was more of a wreck than the last one, still studded with chunks of cement and pieces of what Daniel assumed used to be walls. He had come across a piece of wallpaper and a broken coffee cup, and even though he knew most buildings were uninhabited when their owners set fire to them to collect insurance money, it was still depressing work.

More practically, they were going to have to figure out a way to get the city to haul away the debris that was too big to put in a trash can, but in the meantime, he was piling it in a corner of the lot. With any luck, the ground would be clear enough to plant some trees in the fall. Meanwhile, this would keep Daniel busy and entertained. Someone in one of the neighboring buildings had the habit of watching *Soul Train* at top volume with the window open every afternoon, so at least there was often something good to listen to while he worked.

CHAPTER EIGHTEEN

"It looks less bad than last time."

Daniel looked up to see Alex grimly surveying the site. "Hey. This is a nice surprise."

"I left work a little early and thought I'd come collect you for once."

Daniel pulled off his gloves and wiped the sweat off his forehead. He had been working outside since early afternoon and was a sweaty mess. "You want to hang around while I shower and then we can go make some dinner at your place?"

Alex picked up Daniel's thermos and portable radio while Daniel locked his equipment in a makeshift shed that somebody in the neighborhood had built at the end of the lot and which was going to be the pretense for the cops to start making trouble. But the alternative was either hauling all his gear the three blocks back to his apartment every day or having his shovel and radio stolen more often than he wanted to replace them. Bored kids would steal damn near anything. They stole things, threw their sneakers over telephone wires, and had a knack for finding the least boring music.

Daniel was back to feeling very old again.

He peeled off his grimy clothes as soon as he stepped foot in his apartment. "Make yourself at home," he told Alex, and then got in the shower before the water had heated up, but after the heat of the day, the blast of cool water was a relief. He could hear Alex puttering around in the kitchen—one of the weirder downsides to having a shower in the kitchen was the sense of doing something private in the middle of the house, which he supposed was exactly what he was doing.

"There's an empty lot around the corner from my building," Alex said when Daniel was rummaging around in his bedroom for clean clothes.

"Do you mean the one on 5th?"

"Yeah, and I think it connects with another lot on 4th."

"Huh." Daniel had been wanting to get his hands on a lot that went through like that, mainly because he liked the idea of a secret passage between streets, but also because it would get terrific light. "I wonder if anyone over there has their eye on it." He had met a handful of other people in the neighborhood who were doing what he was doing with empty lots, and had heard of a few others.

With his toe, Alex nudged the pile of dirty laundry that lived in the corner of Alex's bedroom. Alex's own laundry went into a wicker hamper situated in the corner of his tidy bedroom.

"You've been spending four nights a week at my apartment," Alex said.

"At least," Daniel said, pulling on some jeans. Overnight visits had been folded into the routine he and Alex already had. On nights Daniel was staying out late, he slept at his own apartment. Other nights he stayed with Alex. He'd basically been treating his own apartment like a combination between an office, a changing room, an a by-the-hour motel, and he was pretty sure that the reason he was down to one clean T-shirt here was that the rest were at Alex's.

He had been worried at first that Alex wouldn't be able to sleep with Daniel there, but that turned out not to be much of a problem. If Daniel wasn't ready to sleep, he either read on the sofa or sat at the kitchen table, sketching out notes for whatever article he was drafting. It was all working better than he had hoped for.

Well, for Daniel at least. He thought about the new mattress, the sheets. He looked up at Alex, but his face didn't reveal anything. "Want me to start sleeping here a bit more?" Daniel asked, trying to sound casual, off-hand.

He expected Alex to give him an answer, because he always did. That was how their friendship worked.

"Is that what you want?" Alex asked. Daniel stared at him.

"I asked you first," Daniel said, because apparently he was six years old now.

"Daniel." Alex sat on the edge of the bed and looked up at him.

"What's that supposed to mean?"

"It means that you get a say."

"It's your apartment."

Alex shot him an unimpressed look. "You think I don't know that I can ask you to sleep at your own apartment? I could probably ask you to sleep in the gutter. You never say no to me."

That wasn't true, but it wasn't far from the truth, either. "I like making you happy."

"You could give me a chance to make you happy too. And right now I want to know if you mind staying at my apartment. I don't want to stay at yours very often."

Daniel replayed the last few minutes of conversation. "Are you trying to sort out the logistics of where we sleep? Together?"

"'Trying' is the operative word, Daniel. I might even succeed if you told me your preferences."

Daniel's face was hot for reasons he didn't understand, and he didn't know where to look. "I don't need to spend any more time at my apartment than I currently do. I don't miss it or anything."

Alex was quiet, apparently interested in studying a loose thread on the bedspread. For a moment Daniel thought Alex would ask for more confirmation, for more clarification, when all Daniel could think was that he'd take as much of Alex's time as he could get, but that in this instance, as with most instances, he was happy to let Alex's preferences guide them both. It was just—he hadn't expected Alex to want more of him. He had never expected Alex to fling open the door to his life any wider than he already had, and now that this seemed to be happening, Daniel didn't know how to react.

"Then you should probably wash this laundry and bring a few more changes of clothing to my apartment," Alex finally said. "And a razor, because you ruin mine when you use it."

"Are you sure?"

"I cut myself on the chin the last time you borrowed it," Alex said darkly. "You're asking a lot of a razor when you expect it to cut through all that." With a disapproving frown that Daniel might take seriously if Alex weren't in the habit of rubbing against his jaw like a cat, Alex gestured at Daniel's week of stubble, which was about another week away from being a proper beard. He'd probably shave tomorrow.

"No, I mean, you don't have to ask me to stay over because you think that's what I want. You can tell me that you need time to yourself. I'm not going to take it personally. I just—I worry about getting in your hair. Getting on your nerves."

"Everything gets on my nerves. *I* get on my nerves. If I need time to myself, I know by now that I can trust you to leave me alone, even if you're in the same room. Daniel, I—never mind, it's stupid."

"No way, I'm not going to be the only one here sounding stupid."

Alex sighed. "Sometimes when you aren't there, I'm annoyed about it."

CHAPTER EIGHTEEN

Daniel stared at him and then started laughing. Alex rolled his eyes and turned pink.

"No, no," Daniel said. "It's just—that would have been 'I miss you' from anybody else."

Alex gave him an incredulous look. "Do you need me to tell you that?"

"No," Daniel said, which was the truth, but he felt flustered by the question. He didn't need Alex to say that sort of thing. But he didn't mind it, either. "I don't need—of course not. I'm not asking for—"

"Of course you're not asking for anything. You never are. But didn't you know that I miss you when you aren't around? I thought I was already being too obvious. I always feel obvious around you."

"Oh," Daniel said.

"Daniel, I don't like saying that I miss you, because I don't want you to take it as a request. I don't want you to clear your schedule to entertain me."

"I wouldn't do that," Daniel said. Although—he might. He couldn't say for sure that he wouldn't, actually. "I, okay, I might."

"It wasn't a complaint. I know you want to make me happy, and how could I not love that about you? It just means I need to be careful about what I ask."

Daniel suddenly wished he had on a shirt, even one of the dirty shirts from the laundry pile, because he felt doubly exposed with Alex saying all this, his voice as matter-of-fact as ever, as if pointing out that Daniel would do anything for him was just as unremarkable as noticing the weather. It's not that Daniel thought it was exactly a secret, but he didn't know how to think about it being out in the open.

"And I don't like saying that sort of thing," Alex went on. "I say I love you, you have to say it back. I say I miss you, you have to say it back. It feels—I don't know. It feels unnecessary, because you already know those things. Or at least I thought you did."

"I know you love me," Daniel said.

"Do you, though?" Alex sounded fully exasperated now.

"Yes. You do make it obvious. It's just that you can love someone and not want to spend all your time with them."

"Who's talking about all their time? We both have jobs and lives. I'm talking about you moving in with me."

"You're—what?"

Alex winced. "I wasn't going to say anything yet, but I don't know how to make this clearer, so maybe now is just as well. When my lease is up in November, I'm going to find a bigger apartment. That way there's enough space for you to work in one room, or for me to have quiet. I don't know. It just seems like an extra room would be a good idea. To be clear, I'm doing that even if you don't want to move in with me. It's an open invitation. And, for what it's worth, I don't care if you keep this apartment. I don't care if you spend half your nights here. I know you have friends here, and the garden. Your rent is a pittance, which is still more than it's worth, but—"

Daniel kissed him, and only partly because he didn't think he could hear any more without crying or otherwise embarrassing himself.

Chapter Nineteen

"Did you know that the city charges for block party permits?" Daniel asked. It was ninety degrees and they were sitting against a wall in a shady part of the garden, very carefully not moving. Blanca had declared it too hot for weed, which was all Daniel needed to know about the severity of the heat wave.

"The city charges for everything," responded Blanca. "Tell me you didn't just learn that today."

"And they charge even more for a temporary liquor license."

"Don't get one of those," Blanca interjected. "We'll keep the booze in a cooler in the front hall."

The garden looked good, or at least as good as any garden was ever going to look at the end of a brutally hot August. Some neighbors had developed a schedule to take turns weeding the communal spaces. The plots Daniel had put in along the south wall were filled with herbs and small, dangerous-looking peppers. Blanca was feeling justifiably smug about her plan having worked, and the people in the neighborhood who contributed knowledge and plants were pleased to see an actual functioning garden.

When Daniel looked at the garden, he didn't see any traces

of the empty lot that had been there when he moved in two years earlier. It had been rough. *He* had been rough. And now the empty lot was a garden and he was...he was okay. He was happy. It was possible that this garden was the first thing he had accomplished in his life. It felt like a lucky talisman. Every time he walked past it he couldn't help but feel good, because if something so derelict had become something good just through the combined effort of a handful of people, then there was hope for everything else.

And so Daniel wanted to have a party. Or, rather, he wanted to organize a neighborhood party. In an ideal world, they could have had a party during Labor Day weekend, which was only two days away, but the heat wave was going to chase everyone out of the city who had a place to go, and would have everybody else running in the direction of the nearest fountain or fire hydrant. So they'd do it the following weekend, which had the advantage of giving Daniel time to get a block party permit.

"Miriam's trying to organize the tenants to buy the building from the landlord," Blanca said. "Thought you should hear it from me first."

Daniel went still. "The building is going to be a co-op? Won't that mean that anyone who can't afford to buy their apartment will get evicted?" He had heard of landlords demanding cash from tenants and of banks refusing loans.

"The landlord owes back taxes to the city, which, according to Miriam, means he'll be eager to get this building off his hands. Nobody needs to be evicted if we do this right, if we do this before the landlord decides to initiate the process himself."

And, okay, it was true that most of the stories Daniel had heard involved landlords who converted their buildings into co-ops as a last-ditch effort to squeeze some money out of them.

"All right," Daniel said, trying to keep an open mind. "Tell me more."

"We only need fifteen percent agreement among tenants. Miriam says thirty-five percent gives us more flexibility, though."

"A third of the units are unoccupied. How does that change things?"

"Only occupied units count."

"What about mortgages?"

"No," said Blanca. "Assume that nobody here is qualifying for any loans."

"Right. Okay. So everybody needs to pay cash. Who here has that kind of cash?"

"First of all, it's going to cost less than you think. The landlord couldn't sell this building if he tried. Market value is just this side of a goose egg. Miriam says two thousand dollars, tops."

Well, shit. That was only a bit more than two years' rent. Still. "How many people have two thousand dollars lying around, though?"

"Miriam and I do. You do. Mrs. Navarro. Mr. Antoine, probably. That's thirty-five percent right there."

Mrs. Navarro had lived in unit 4C for over twenty years, had raised her children there and currently had one of her grandchildren living with her. Mr. Antoine had been there even longer. "What is it without me?"

"It's still over fifteen percent."

"Okay. And then later on people can still buy their apartments from the co-op, right?"

"Miriam says we can come up with a rent-to-own plan for

tenants who are interested. Daniel, we can do whatever we want."

About an hour ago he had been planning on moving in with Alex, and only hanging on to his apartment as a place to work if he was feeling especially nocturnal and to serve as a convenient home base for future gardens.

He definitely hadn't considered buying either it or anything else. One of the things he liked best about this apartment was that he could easily afford it doing work he loved. Buying it, even if it would be as cheap as Blanca thought, would probably wipe out his meager savings.

Also, he didn't love the idea of co-ops. Landlords should just fucking do their job and keep buildings habitable. But after hearing what Blanca said, now he was worried that their landlord was going to try to unload this building one way or another. So many buildings in their neighborhood had been abandoned—the landlord evicted everyone and then either torched it or let the property be seized by the city for back taxes. And when either of those things happened, the neighborhood got one step closer to not existing anymore. According to the older residents, it was already nothing like it had been ten, fifteen, years earlier. Neighborhoods changed, of course they did, but this neighborhood was in danger of being wiped clean off the map.

Blanca and Miriam's way was probably the best for everyone. It was better than anyone getting evicted; it was better than the building getting torched or abandoned.

When he thought about this building getting burned to the ground, becoming another empty lot filled with the broken detritus of people's lives, he was furious. He really didn't go in for anger; people had been telling him for his entire life that he was mild mannered to a fault. But he had put work into this neighborhood and he wasn't letting it get taken away from anyone.

A very practical voice that sounded like Alex pointed out that this neighborhood was—not good, to put it charitably, and it was getting worse. The only reason this building could become a co-op was that it was effectively worthless. But that was value as measured by income, not value as measured by the worth of a home.

And this building *was* his home, as was this neighborhood. It had welcomed him—well, no, the East Village had probably never welcomed anyone. It had been the only place that made sense to him when he moved here. The neighborhood had been as ragged as he was, as caught between the past and the future, as damaged by the trials of a world far wider than lower Manhattan.

Even if just Miriam, Blanca, Mrs. Navarro, and Mr. Antoine bought in, that would be enough. But Daniel would bring the numbers to thirty-five percent, which made things safer—at least, that was his understanding. He needed to talk to Miriam to make sure. He needed to talk to his father, who knew more about housing law than anybody needed to.

He needed to talk to Alex.

"There's one other way," Blanca said, "but Miriam hates it."

"Oh?"

"We let everyone get evicted, let the landlord abandon the building, and then just…take it over."

"You mean buy it from the city?"

"Maybe. Or we just…move in."

That was illegal, but not necessarily any more or less illegal than what he was doing with the gardens. Cops in this city had enough to keep them busy without looking too closely into who had the deed to a building.

"Mrs. Navarro isn't going to live in an illegal squat," Daniel said, returning to reality. "Honestly, if people want to live in a squat, there are probably twenty buildings between here and Tompkins Square Park that they can take their pick from. I'll even show them how to st—how to borrow water and electricity. But that doesn't need to happen here." The more he talked, the surer he felt.

"Okay," Blanca said. "Should I tell Miriam you're in?"

"Yeah," Daniel said. "Tell her I'm in."

* * *

Every August for the past sixteen years, Alex was surprised anew by how disgusting New York managed to become. He always thought it had reached the maximum possible levels of horror in July, but no, the end of August was worse.

Something had gone wrong with garbage collection and a few days' worth of accumulated trash cluttered the sidewalks and, encouraged by the heat wave, smelled like death. Alex had stopped paying attention to whether this was caused by a strike or some other confusion, because on principle, he didn't want to be cross with striking workers, but in reality, he could not shut up the superstitious part of his brain that shouted that they were all going to die of cholera or malaria or something if this garbage didn't get taken away. The piles of trash weren't as high as they had been during the strike five or six years ago, at least.

Between the oppressive heat and the garbage, the sidewalks were unnavigable, subways were as bad as they ever were in

August, cabs were impossible to find, and periodic storms soaked the city in a layer of rain that did nothing to wash away the grime or dissipate the heat. Throughout the city, people popped the caps on fire hydrants so kids could at least get some relief. The fountain in Washington Square Park was filled with people who were likely going to catch appalling fungal infections from one another, but Alex could hardly judge them.

"I need soup," Alex said. It was the Friday of Labor Day weekend and he and Daniel were spread out on Alex's bed, not touching, not moving, the air conditioner operating on full blast. Con Edison was threatening to reduce voltage because of too many air conditioners operating at once, but Alex only felt a momentary pang of guilt for contributing to the problem.

"Ice cream," Daniel countered. He was only wearing underwear, and the fact that Alex wasn't even tempted by the sight really said something.

"After the soup."

"Tell me you mean gazpacho or something. It's ninety-five degrees. It's not soup weather."

"The hotter the day, the hotter the soup." Alex tried to deliver this with authority, in the same voice he (unsuccessfully) employed to try to persuade Daniel to take vitamins, put zinc oxide on his nose before working outside, and avoid being around cigarette smoke.

"Well, that sounds deranged."

"It works. Look, worst case scenario is that you go with me to get soup and it's horrible, but you come back here and feel better as soon as you step into the apartment."

They went to Leshkos and drank hot borscht and Alex told himself he already felt cooler, or at least less close to death.

"My building is going co-op," Daniel said.

"So is the building next to mine," Alex said. "I can't decide how I feel about it."

"I mean," Daniel said, looking very interested in his spoon, "that I'm going to buy my apartment."

"You could probably buy six of your apartments for the cost of that bowl of soup."

Daniel didn't say anything, and for a moment the only sound was the whir and rattle of an oscillating fan in the corner of the restaurant and the muted clatter of dishes being washed in the kitchen.

"You wouldn't mind?" Daniel asked. He looked up from his spoon, but there was something off in his expression.

"If I'm supposed to mind, you're going to need to spell it out for me."

"I'm not going to move in with you."

"I got that part."

"I mean, I still want to stay with you most nights, just like we do now. I just like my neighborhood and my neighbors. It's the first place that's ever been mine."

"If you buy it, can you put in better windows? Drywall? A real bathroom?"

"You really don't mind?"

"Didn't I just tell you that I don't mind? I know I did. Can the co-op fees be used to hire an electrician to rewire the building?"

"I'll ask Miriam," Daniel said, smiling into his empty bowl.

"How are you going to buy it?" This was probably too blunt, but as far as Alex knew, Daniel didn't have extra money just sitting around, and he didn't think banks were in the business of giving mortgages for the purchase of half-decimated tenements in Alphabet City.

"The *Rolling Stone* article," Daniel said. "And maybe the one for *Esquire* last winter."

Daniel had said a dozen times that he liked to live off the money he made from his music reviews, meaning the pieces he wrote for the *Village Voice*. It hadn't occurred to Alex that Daniel might be saving the money from everything else, or that those two magazine articles added up to enough to buy an apartment. Then again, it really was a terrible apartment.

There was something odd playing around the edges of Daniel's expression, and even though by now Alex had a relatively easy time reading his face, there was something new there alongside the air of apologetic regret that always accompanied Daniel disappointing anyone. He seemed—pleased, maybe. Pleased with himself? He was proud, and he should be.

Daniel had been barely functional when he moved into this neighborhood. He had been sent overseas against his will, then sent back home, and the fact that that could happen had disrupted either his faith in a smooth-running world or his interest in it. And so he had claimed a tiny corner of that world for himself and set about making it better in one specific way.

It wasn't so different than what Alex was doing: he couldn't do much about the state of the universe, but he could make sure kids and their parents had a good doctor who spoke their language and who didn't charge more than they could afford.

Alex weighed his words carefully. "It would have been nice to have you around every morning. I don't want you to think that I'm secretly relieved that you aren't moving in with me. But it'll be just as nice to have you around whenever you are around. Congratulations," Alex said. "I'm happy for you. And I'm proud of you."

"You really are, aren't you."

"Do I say things I don't mean?" Alex didn't even mean it as a rhetorical question; he was just confused that Daniel seemed to have gotten him confused with someone who spoke in riddles.

"Never," Daniel said. "You never do."

Chapter Twenty

The heat wave broke with buckets of rain, so they spent Labor Day Sunday holed up in Alex's apartment watching grainy westerns on the television. Daniel was considering whether he had the energy to get up and make sandwiches when the phone rang.

Alex answered, and then carried on a conversation in Ukrainian, which wouldn't have been unusual if he hadn't also been holding the phone between his ear and his shoulder while trying to get his shoes on. Daniel turned the television off and got his own shoes on too, reasoning that whatever was about to take Alex out into the pouring rain, he might want company.

"It's my sister," Alex said when he hung up. "Or, rather, it's Larysa. She has a fever and a rash, and Polyna can't get in touch with their pediatrician."

"A bad fever?"

"Not so high that she needs to go to the hospital, but high enough that Polyna has been trying ice baths."

Daniel was faintly horrified by the idea of tiny Larysa in an ice bath. "So you're going to Brooklyn?"

"No, I told her to drive into the city and meet me at the clinic.

That'll be faster." He walked toward the door, hesitating when he noticed Daniel following. "Are you going home? You know you can wait here."

"I'll keep you company. Besides, you know what parking is like. Polyna probably won't want to spend any time circling the block, so she can just hop out with the baby and I'll park the car."

They probably didn't need to rush, because it took over forty minutes to drive into the city from Brighton Beach, even when there wasn't traffic. But Alex wouldn't keep any patient waiting in the rain, and certainly not his sister and niece. So when they got to the clinic, Daniel got to watch Alex putter around the exam room, doing things that nurses usually did—laying out tongue depressors, a thermometer, one of those ear flashlights, whatever they were called, as well as the smallest blood pressure cuff Alex had ever seen.

"Are rashes dangerous in babies?" Daniel asked.

"The short answer is no. Probably every infant has a rash and a fever together at some point. There's chicken pox, measles, roseola, rubella, fifth disease, mumps, and that's not even getting into the rashes that just go along with other infections for no real reason. But even common illnesses can have complications, and that's what we watch out for." As he spoke, he washed his hands and rolled up his sleeves.

Daniel went to the waiting room to look out the window for Polyna's car. When it finally rolled up, it wasn't just Alex's sister and niece in the car. His nephew was there too, and so was Mrs. Savchenko.

"Stepan was in a mood and wouldn't be left behind," Polyna told Alex as he held the umbrella for her and Daniel slid into the driver's seat. And sure enough, the five-year-old looked like he had spent the car ride crying. Mrs. Savchenko, evidently brought along to look after the sick baby during the car ride, looked precisely the way Alex looked after a long day.

Daniel parked the car around the corner and managed to get back to the clinic without getting soaked. When he pushed the door open, he found Stepan sitting in the waiting room, his arms crossed over his chest and refusing to look at his grandmother.

"I want to read the dinosaur book," Stepan said plaintively.

"The dinosaur book is at home," said Mrs. Savchenko, exuding weariness from every pore.

"But I want to read the dinosaur book."

"We have a dinosaur book," Daniel said, rummaging through the basket of children's books Alex and Mary kept in the waiting room. He found it and held it aloft in triumph.

Stepan scowled. "That book is for babies."

"Oh, right," Daniel said, dropping the book back into the basket. "Of course it is. What kind of information do you find in, um, grown-up dinosaur books?"

"My book has a picture of a stegosaurus. A realistic picture, not a cartoon," Stepan added, because this was apparently an important point. "The stegosaurus is an herbivore but most books try to make it look scary. My book doesn't."

Daniel sat beside Stepan and, out of the corner of his eye, saw Mrs. Savchenko slip out of the waiting room and into the exam room. "What color is the stegosaurus?" Daniel asked, because he didn't have many dinosaur-based conversational gambits at his disposal.

"In my book, it's brown, but we don't know for sure what color it was."

"No? Why not?"

The look that passed over Stepan's face was identical to the look his uncle got when Daniel skipped a meal or smelled like cigarettes: mingled sorrow and dismay at Daniel's incapacity. "Because we only have fossils, Uncle Daniel. That means old bones that have turned into rock. And you can't tell what color something is from its bones. Why are you wet?"

Daniel explained that he had gotten rained on while walking back from where he parked Stepan's mother's car. The question, he noted, had been why Daniel was wet, not why Daniel was there in the first place. Daniel had been appearing at Alex's side for as long as this child could probably remember.

Polyna's kids were the only people likely to ever call him uncle, and it pleased Daniel that it had happened in the first place, because this child—so like his Uncle Alex—had made it happen. Whenever Daniel looked at Stepan—with his wheat-blond hair and his supercilious little expression and his air of being perpetually on the verge of some horrible change in mood as soon as someone broke a rule only Stepan knew about—he suspected he had a glimpse into what Alex had been like at that age.

"I don't know much about dinosaurs," Daniel lamented. And then he was hit with inspiration. "I bet a lot of the facts in the baby book would be new to me. I wonder if you could read it." He knew from Alex's bragging that Stepan could sound out most words, and decided to bet that he also recognized dinosaur names.

When everybody else came back into the waiting room, Stepan was painstakingly reading the dinosaur book to Daniel. Daniel glanced up long enough to assure himself that all three of the adults looked reassured, and nobody seemed to be hurrying out the door to any hospitals or drugstores.

"It's roseola," Alex said when Stepan cast the dinosaur book aside in favor of examining his sister's rash. "Nothing to worry about. Tylenol, fluids, the usual."

Daniel went and got the car, and when he pulled up in front of the clinic, Stepan insisted on shaking his hand, which was really fucking adorable but Daniel managed to be serious about it, shaking the kid's hand as solemnly as a congressman greeting one of his constituents. After he had packed the kid into the car, Alex put his hand on Daniel's back. It was the kind of thing he did a dozen times a day, but not in front of his family—usually not in front of anybody other than Mary.

Daniel looked up at him and raised his eyebrows, thinking he ought to give Alex a heads up that he was breaking one of his own unspoken rules. But Alex just slid his hand over until his arm was fully around Daniel's waist, and with his other hand waved goodbye to his family.

And then they headed in the direction of the Chinese restaurant, as if nothing were different, and Daniel supposed nothing actually was different—it was just Alex settling in more comfortably. For Alex, though, that sort of comfort was something of a luxury; it was hard won.

Daniel smiled so much at dinner that Alex put a hand on his forehead to check for a fever.

* * *

"What I'm saying," Daniel said, "is that I can have more than one home."

"I'm not disagreeing with you," Alex said, not really clear what Daniel thought he was going on about.

"It's just—the apartment is my home, even if I don't sleep

there much. And your apartment—your new apartment, or wherever you are—is also my home."

"Right. Like dual citizenship."

"Yes!"

It was clear that Daniel was working something out for himself, but in Alex's opinion, he was overcomplicating it. "Look, any home I have is yours by default, regardless of however many other homes you have."

Daniel blinked and then got this goofy smile that usually meant Alex had accidentally done something sweet.

"Come on," Alex said. "We'll be late."

"There's no such thing as late to a block party."

This did nothing to reassure Alex, because that likely meant this was going to involve loud music and too many people he hadn't ever met. To be fair, that was probably the definition of party. But also to be fair, Alex hated parties.

Daniel had told him a dozen times he didn't need to go, and of course Alex knew that. He wasn't planning to stay, obviously. He was going to say hello to Daniel's neighbors and then leave before anybody started to break the law.

But when they got there, the music was only moderately loud and a full third of the people gathered in the street were older than Alex. He recognized the extremely elderly Haitian man who lived on the ground floor and the Puerto Rican woman who brought her grandchild to the clinic. There was Blanca, dancing semi-provocatively with one of the old men from across the street; a teenager he recognized as one of the boys who helped Daniel with more physically demanding gardening jobs; and Miriam, who was helping herself to what looked like a plate of potato salad from a table at which a pair of middle-aged women stood sentry—whether protecting the food from flies

CHAPTER TWENTY

or some other danger, Alex could not tell.

The street itself was blocked off from traffic—not that there was ever much traffic in this neighborhood—and some children were playing in the street, engaged in a game that Alex couldn't identify, and which they might have been making up as they went along. Lawn chairs were scattered along the sidewalks. Someone had set up a turntable—it wasn't Daniel's, Alex was surprised to note—and the record playing was actually something that Alex recognized. He had expected something jarring and difficult to listen to, but he supposed that the number of non-teenagers was large enough to exert some influence and the resulting compromise was Gladys Knight and the Pips.

Daniel was still by Alex's side despite the fact that he had to be longing to go say hello to people.

"Go," Alex said. He wouldn't have come at all if he thought Daniel would spend the whole time babysitting him. "Seriously, go."

Alex watched Daniel slot himself into a conversation with a handful of people Alex didn't recognize. Then Alex helped himself to an empanada and a bottle of beer and headed off toward the garden. From the bench, he could still see some of the party and hear the music, but it wasn't so loud and there was little danger of him attracting the well-meaning attention of someone who thought that anyone standing alond must need company.

Alex had no idea what the names were of any of the plants that surrounded him, despite Daniel having explained it more than once. Plants just simply hadn't been a factor for him when he was growing up or in fact at any point in his life before he met Daniel, and therefore, that entire category of information refused to assemble itself into actual knowledge within Alex's mind. Maybe because of his total ignorance, he was able to sit amidst the plants and just think of them as...pretty. As pretty little things that Daniel had put there, and that notion made him happier than any plant taxonomy could.

"They're ferns," Miriam said, coming to sit beside Alex.

"Hmm?"

"The plants you were looking at. They're ferns. Blanca took cuttings or something from in front of her allergist's office on Lexington."

Miriam was Alex's favorite of Daniel's friends. She could be relied on to either sit quietly or, if prompted with a question on one of her favorite topics, gently hold forth about the criminal justice system or industrial agriculture in a way that didn't require much participation from her audience and which never failed to briefly convince Alex that he ought to try vegetarianism or something equally unlikely.

Today, though, she seemed to be content to sit quietly as they ate, and then to offer Alex a joint that materialized out of nowhere. He declined, content with his beer. As far as neighbors went, she was close to Alex's ideal.

It occurred to him that something like Daniel's inane transitive property of friendship might actually apply in this case. What Alex had said about Daniel having a home with him, by default, worked in both directions; these people were perhaps his neighbors for the sole reason that they belonged to Daniel. Daniel had made this his home, and maybe that made it Alex's too. Alex had known a number of homes, and the idea of acquiring another one—not because he was forced to leave his old home, but because he had been welcomed into a new one—did not displease him.

CHAPTER TWENTY

The wail of police sirens—or, more likely, fire engines—sounded from uptown, and in response, someone turned up the music. This had the predictable response of encouraging dancing, and before the song was over, Alex saw Daniel and Blanca dancing in a way that might, a few months ago, have made Alex jealous. But now, seeing them obviously enjoy one another, it just made him—happy. It made him uncomplicatedly happy in the way that the plants did, in the way that Daniel's shampoo in his shower did. In the way that Daniel did.

Some people were like that, Alex supposed. They shed happiness like plants released pollen.

It surprised him, still, these instances of unlooked-for joy, these unlikely places where happiness took up root. Maybe at some point he'd get used to the sensation of encountering something unexpected and lovely—a sensation that seemed to go hand in hand with having a life with Daniel Cabot. Maybe a decade from now, maybe three decades from now, he'd come across some completely neutral reminder of Daniel's existence—a tube of fruit-flavored toothpaste, say—and regard it without something peculiar happening in his chest, but he doubted it.

In a little bit, Alex would go inside and take refuge in Daniel's apartment. Maybe he'd read; maybe he'd make a list of what Daniel needed at the store. Later, much later, Daniel would come inside and offer to go back to Alex's for the night, but they would stay here, wrapped in sheets that likely cost more than anything else in the apartment. They'd listen to the sound of kids setting off firecrackers and their parents dancing to salsa music. Blanca's laughter would echo through the stairwell as Miriam finally coaxed her up to bed, and the sound of a

Spanish lullaby would drift through the open window from the grandmother on the fourth floor.

And then tomorrow Alex would go to Bloomingdale's with Daniel's mother, and the day after that he was going to visit an honest-to-god townhouse that Mary and Paul were thinking of buying. The following weekend he and Daniel would go out to Brighton Beach for Alex's father's sixtieth birthday, and Daniel would manage to orchestrate it so they left before Alex was ready to walk into the sea.

They were all tiny sparks of joy, like those fireflies he had seen a few months earlier, and Alex didn't quite know how his life had become so full of them, but he knew Daniel had something to do with it.

THE END

If you enjoyed this book, you might also enjoy Peter Cabot Gets Lost or Tommy Cabot Was Here.

Acknowledgments

This book was supposed to be a novella of twenty-five thousand words. Four weeks later it was this, and I had learned the valuable life lesson that I can write very quickly if I pretend it's not happening. For this miracle of productivity, I have to thank everyone in the Write What You May discord for collectively insisting that Writing Is Fun (dammit). I also have to thank the collective wisdom in that discord for help with the title, typo-spotting, and various publishing questions that I somehow had never figured out.

Daniel's apartment is a very real apartment I lived in on East Sixth Street many years ago. Once my ceiling caved in. Everyone who came over was positive there were ghosts. The door had over ten locks and there was indeed a shower in the kitchen. Despite all this, the vibes of the place were, somehow, amazing and I cried real tears when I moved out. Is it strange to acknowledge a (terrible) apartment? Who cares, I'm doing it anyway.

My parents were invaluable sources of information regarding New York in the seventies even though they laughed in my face when I asked how people deposited checks before ATMs existed.

I'm so grateful for the friends who shared their experiences as first and second generation Ukrainian and Chinese immigrants. I grew up with several people in these communities but that doesn't substitute for direct knowledge, and I'm very grateful for their candor. Any inaccuracies, are, of course, my own.

Alex's anxiety, sensory processing issues, relationship to touch, and need to decompress in solitude are taken from my own experiences. He's autistic, though; I'm not. I'm grateful for the help that autistic family and friends provided in rounding out Alex's character. Again, any inaccuracies are all my own.

A million thanks to Kim Runciman for copy editing and proofreading this, and to Bran at Crowglass Designs for the cover.

Most of all, I have to thank the readers who've enjoyed the Cabot series. I'm so glad there's an audience for books about people who don't do much of anything except wear sweaters (or, in this case, band t-shirts) and cry. I love writing these books, I love hearing about people for whom they are comfort reads, and I hope you all enjoy this book too.

About the Author

Cat Sebastian writes queer historical romances. Cat's books have received starred reviews from Kirkus, Publishers Weekly, Library Journal, and Booklist, and she's been featured in the *Washington Post, Entertainment Weekly*, and Jezebel.

Before writing, Cat was a lawyer and a teacher and did a variety of other jobs she liked much less than she enjoys writing happy endings for queer people. She was born in New Jersey and lived in New York and Arizona before settling down in a swampy part of south. When she isn't writing, she's probably reading, having one-sided conversations with her dog, or doing the crossword puzzle.

The best way to keep up with Cat's projects is to visit her website or subscribe to her newsletter.

You can connect with me on:
- https://catsebastian.com
- https://twitter.com/CatSWrites
- https://instagram.com/CatSWrites

Subscribe to my newsletter:
- https://mailchi.mp/7c28043ac649/catsebastian

Also by Cat Sebastian

The Cabots:
Tommy Cabot Was Here
Peter Cabot Gets Lost
Daniel Cabot Puts Down Roots

London Highwaymen:
The Queer Principles of Kit Webb
The Perfect Crimes of Marian Hayes

Page & Sommers:
Hither, Page
The Missing Page

The Sedgwicks:
It Takes Two to Tumble
A Gentleman Never Keeps Score
Two Rogues Make a Right

The Turners:
The Soldier's Scoundrel
The Lawrence Browne Affair
The Ruin of a Rake
A Little Light Mischief

Regency Impostors:
Unmasked by the Marquess
A Duke in Disguise
A Delicate Deception